MY AUNT, THE VAMPIRE

A SAPPHIC VAMPIRE ROMANCE

AUTUMN WOLFF

CHAPTER 1

Steel rattled against rusted iron and my wrist as I pulled on the old radiator pipe for the 50th time. My wrist stung as the handcuffs tore into my skin and let loose more blood. The pain was minimal, and I was probably going to need a tetanus shot or something. If I developed lockjaw, I'm sure my captors would call their faith healer to pray over me until fever finally took me.

Though that would be a sweet mercy, I thought, glumly, watching the thin line of red pool at the bottom of my wrist and drip to the floor.

The room that I'd called home for the last two days was empty, except for an old blanket I'd been given to sleep on and a plate with crackers and salami I hadn't touched. My stomach was caving in on itself, and hunger pains shot through my abdomen. But I didn't trust the latest food I'd been given.

Hard to trust anything when you spend your days handcuffed to various things, an old dresser bolted to the wall in a church basement, a doorknob in a remote cabin, or the back of a condemned rec center that people hadn't used in years.

My captors moved me around if they suspected there was a chance of someone accidentally finding me. That'd been my life for the last month.

Looking up, I felt a drop of water fall from the dilapidated ceiling onto my forehead. Was it raining outside?

"Great. . . maybe this room will flood and finally put me out of my misery," I mumbled.

My skin was grimy. I hadn't had a proper shower in god knows how long. Wet wipes only keep you clean for so long.

The man guarding me tonight was supposed to bring my chamber pot back in, not that using it ever got less mortifying. But I hadn't seen or heard him in an hour.

"If he doesn't hurry, I'm going to have to decide which end of the radiator would be less disgusting to piss on," I said, straining my ears toward the locked door, hoping to hear him returning.

But it was quiet as a. . . well, an abandoned building.

So, I crossed my legs, begged my bladder to be

patient, and placed my back against the wall. Nothing to do but play my favorite game. I made it myself. The game was called How Will I Kill My Grandfather When I Get Free? I was still working on the name. It was a little long.

But hey, thanks to that nutjob cult leader, or "pastor" as he called himself, I had all the time I needed to sit and refine my game.

Maybe I can sell the rights to those guys who made Cards Against Humanity, I thought. *They make weird shit.*

I'd be a millionaire before I even graduated high school. Maybe they'd even make a movie. Vedalia, the 17-year-old who was taken from her parents and chained in a basement for a month but escaped to become a successful tabletop game designer.

There was just one problem as far as I could see. Two, if you counted the name I had to fix. I still needed to get loose, and this goddamn radiator didn't seem all that sympathetic to my plan. Neither did the chipped tile my sore ass was sitting on.

In fact, nothing in this room appeared ready to help me escape this nightmare.

Outside, I imagined the moon looking down on the second-most depressing building in Harrison, Arkansas, maybe the third. I dunno. It's not a very pretty town.

So, of course, my grandfather would establish a cult here. And, of course, he'd have a full congregation of nutjobs who believed every single word that flew from his forked tongue. When he wasn't trying to brainwash me, the man was strangely charismatic. Long white hair and a neatly trimmed beard. Carpenter jeans with a blue and white chambray western shirt. Ratty old ballcaps with faded text and logos if he was outdoors. No hats inside.

The man was tall and carried himself as one who was burdened with the task of revealing modern-day prophecy.

But it was his eyes that truly pierced through to your soul. They were a shade of gray-blue that held not an ounce of warmth.

Grandfathers were supposed to be fun, the guys who picked up their grandkids and took them out for donuts and pizza and ice cream, let them run around the park until they passed out. They were supposed to teach you to drive in their old pickup trucks on a dirt road in the middle of nowhere. Grandpa was the one who came over and read to you when you were sick and let you stay up late watching whatever you wanted on TV.

They didn't snatch you away from your mother and father in the middle of the night and restrain you for days on end. They didn't drench you in alleged holy water and preach at you for hours into the night until you were delirious from lack of sleep. They didn't try to drug your food to make you more lethargic and amenable to their brainwashing. But mine did. And I fucking hated him for it.

Yanking on the handcuffs again, I felt my flesh tear more, and blood didn't just drip onto the floor now. It splattered. But I had to get out. I talked a tough game to myself, but the truth was, I was having daily anxiety attacks thanks to how claustrophobic my imprisonment left me. Grandfather couldn't have left me chained up in a scenic mountain valley. No, he had to put me in places that would make even Jigsaw flinch.

And speaking of panic attacks. . . here we went again. My chest constricted, and my heart started to rattle in an obnoxious way that left me feeling as though I might die at any moment. My arms shook uncontrollably, and even my vision started to blur.

It wasn't fair to call this fight or flight because I could do neither. I'd fought the radiator and lost. And there was no flight so long as I was anchored to this goddamn turn-of-the-century furnace.

"Oh god," I thought, slumping against the wall, feeling my breaths come and go faster than they had all day.

Maybe if I banged my head against the wall hard enough I could knock myself out. Can't have a panic attack if you're unconscious, right? Right?

Hyperventilating had all my focus. I tried to think of something else, anything else. But the darkness around me and the inability to move more than three feet in any direction left me mentally crippled.

I might as well have worn an emotional straightjacket.

Sliding down the wall until the only thing not touching the floor was my head, I continued to fight the emptiness and loneliness.

Is this trauma? I thought in between a storm of dread and frenzy. *Or is this just the result of trauma?*

Try as I might to distract myself, my mind wasn't in the right place for a philosophical debate. It can be hard to do that when you feel like you're dying of fright.

My shoulders tightened, and my chest continued to quake uncontrollably.

I was shivering so hard that I didn't hear the door open or notice the woman walking across the room toward me until she was just a few feet away.

I'd say that I jumped, startled by her sudden appearance, but with my inner tension already maxed out, that just wasn't possible. There wasn't any capacity left for an expression of surprise.

"Oh my dear sweet thing," she said, kneeling before me, her Dr. Martens squeaking on the floor as she got closer.

Her voice was husky, and she said a few other things my brain failed to comprehend on account of the inner terror.

The woman before me appeared to be in her 40s

and had ghostly bone-colored skin that looked even paler than my own. And I hadn't seen a lick of sun in the last month.

Her nails were painted a crimson red not unlike the highlights in her soot-colored hair that draped down past her shoulders.

When my eyes focussed long enough to cooperate, I noticed my visitor wore a black leather coat and torn jeans. Her shirt, only partially visible under the jacket, was a plaid button-down.

She kept trying to speak to me, but nothing was getting through. All I could hear was static like an old television with rabbit ears bent too far in one direction or the other.

That's when she got close and locked eyes with me. Her eyes were a deep, inhuman red.

I didn't have trouble understanding her next three words because they went beyond my eyes and sank into my mind. Her pupils seemed to shake as she spoke a single command.

"You are calm," the visitor said.

And. . . son of a bitch, I was calm. Every ounce of adrenaline that'd been working my heart into over-time seemed to vanish in a matter of seconds. I sat up, exhausted from the last few minutes of havoc on my mind and body.

"There you go. All better. Or you will be," she said.

Before I could ask any questions of this stranger,

the man who took my chamber pot returned. He had a gun in his hand. And the thing screwed onto the barrel was a suppressor, I think. He pointed the firearm at my visitor.

"Get the fuck away from her!" he yelled.

His name was Robert. Or maybe Robbie? Something like that. I didn't pay too much attention to the people who kept me bound. . . the people who hung on every word from my grandfather's lips.

My visitor, honest to god hissed, which was a noise I didn't expect as she stood to face the gunman.

"Why don't you put that trinket down before you get hurt?" she said with a tone so cold I felt as though my breath would fog just listening to her speak.

But Robbie or Robert wasn't having it.

"Last warning," he said. "Step away from the girl, or I'll kill you."

And this time, I saw his finger move from the trigger guard to the actual trigger.

"Look — " my visitor started, but she was cut off by rapid gunfire. Robbie was only standing about 15 feet away, and he nailed every shot as I covered my ears.

The movies make you think suppressors entirely silence a gun. But the truth is they're only designed to prevent ear damage if someone isn't wearing plugs or other protection. They're still plenty loud.

I saw every muzzle flash in the dark as Robert unloaded on my visitor, 11 shots in all. She fell backward onto the floor, blood leaking out in every direction as I cried.

The first person who'd showed me a shred of kindness in a month, and, of course, this cult that'd robbed me of everything else had taken that away, too.

When the gunfire stopped, and my ears were still ringing, I screamed at Robbie. No words. No articulation. Just rage pouring out over losing something seconds after I'd received it. . . decency.

"Shut up!" Robert yelled, walking over and kicking my visitor twice to make sure she was dead. "You've got a big day tomorrow, so I'd do a little less screaming and a lot more resting if I were you."

When he was satisfied the woman wasn't going to get up again, he put his gun in the back of his pants and leaned down toward me, smelling of cigarette smoke and cheap beer. Now I knew what he'd been doing for the last hour.

Robert checked my handcuffs and looked at my bleeding wrist.

"Well, I bet that smarts. You smart enough to quit yanking on the cuffs, or are you dumb enough to keep going?"

I wasn't paying attention to his words because I'm pretty sure I heard the sound of something small and metallic falling to the tile. Then another. And another. It sounded like pebbles falling a few inches onto the floor.

But what froze my heart was the sight of my visitor rising once more. And she didn't get up like a human would. She just. . . went from lying flat on her back to right back on her feet. Silent as if an invisible rope had pulled her up.

That shit was scarier than anything I'd seen in "The Nun" or one of those "Insidious" movies. There was no noise. No popping of joints. No rustle of clothing. She just fucking rose quiet as the grave.

Robbie must have been confused by my expression because he paused, cocked his head to the side, and turned around as he stood. But she didn't even let him scream.

The woman tore open his throat, yanking back the man's skull, and drinking deeply like she'd just found water after days under the burning sun.

I froze, but no panic came. I was calm, remember? Or maybe it was more accurate to say I was calmed. I briefly pondered how long that would last.

After a few minutes of this, she let the man's corpse fall to the tile, right next to her blood puddle and 11 spent bullets her body had pushed out and onto the floor.

She licked her lips and then produced a handkerchief from inside the leather jacket. It was a delicate-looking thing and didn't match her aesthetic at all. Her vibe screamed Italian biker.

When she turned to me after cleaning her mouth, I caught sight of her fangs, maybe half an inch longer than the rest of her teeth. Long and sharp enough to pierce flesh, but not so lengthy as to cause problems when she closed her mouth.

"Right. Sorry you had to see that. But I'm going to give you a choice. I overheard Ronald here on the phone a few minutes ago saying they were bringing in an honest-to-good hypnotist tomorrow to brainwash you into their cult. Seems you've been rather stubborn up to this point, and they've grown tired of trying to break your spirit."

Ronald! That's right. His name was Ronald, I thought, rolling my eyes.

I found my voice, but it was quieter than I'd ever heard it before.

"What choice are you going to give me?"

"You can stay here and unwillingly join your grandfather's cult. Or I can take you with me. You ride off into the night on my motorcycle. I even brought you a helmet."

I didn't know this woman, but I knew my grandfather. And that pretty much made the decision for me. But I wanted to clarify a couple of things before leaving with this stranger.

"Who are you?"

"I'm your aunt Becky," she said. "Your mother's older sister."

Wait. My mom had a sister? I never knew that. As

far as I knew, she was an only child like my dad. But then again, I didn't know about my grandfather's cult. So, I guess my life still had a little more room for surprises.

"Are you a — " I was interrupted as Becky smiled.

"Yes."

Well. . . that settled that. I suppose it was a rather stupid question given what I'd just witnessed.

"Am I safe with you?" I asked with, perhaps, a bit more vulnerability than I would've liked. But even if I was calm. . . I was still exhausted and bleeding.

"Do you feel safe right now?" Becky asked.

I thought for a minute, took a deep breath, stared at Ronald's corpse, and made my decision. Like I said, it wasn't all that hard.

"I feel safe. Take me to this super cool vampire bike," I said.

Becky smiled and slowly kneeled, wrapping her fingers gently around the cuff on my bleeding wrist.

She winced a little and then started to pull the double strand and single strand apart. The steel groaned, and then the rivet snapped as the cuff popped open, freeing me.

"How strong are you?" I asked.

"I can flip over a pickup truck with one hand," she said, shrugging like it was no big deal.

Then she pulled out a second handkerchief and motioned to my wrist. I nodded. Becky tenderly wrapped my wound and tied it.

"We'll stop and grab some actual bandages once we're over the state line," she said, helping me stand. My legs were unsteady. But she didn't let me fall.

I locked eyes with her again.

"You're really my mom's sister?"

"Yup. Haven't seen her in a while, but we sent each other letters every few months. I got pictures of you every Christmas, and I sent gifts. I'm not sure if you got any of them, though," she said.

"How come I've never seen you before?" I asked.

The vampire scratched the back of her head. A far-off look of anguish flooded her eyes like she was reliving a series of memories I wasn't privy to.

"Your. . . father made things difficult for my family. And he did that mostly because of your grandfather. It's honestly a long story. And since I have no clue who might have heard Ronald's gunshots, I'd prefer we leave before I have to murder anyone else tonight. I don't want to risk you getting any more hurt than you already are."

I sighed.

"Hard to imagine that being a possibility. But let's get to your bike."

Becky smiled, made sure I could stand on my own, and then led me out into the night air. A crisp autumn wind greeted me, and I shivered a little. I was wearing nothing more than jeans and a robe that was too small for me.

I took a minute to just stand under the quarter

moon, my arms wide, nothing attached to them for the first time in a month. In and out, in and out, in and out, I breathed deep and slow, enjoying the free October air.

When I'd had my fill, Becky led me over to her bike. She'd parked it behind a few bushes that hadn't been trimmed in years. We stood on a quiet street. No cars drove by. The only lights came from a gas station a bit north of us.

Reaching into her saddlebags, Becky pulled out a long-sleeve t-shirt, new jeans, off-brand sneakers, and a new washrag she wet with a water bottle.

I took it and washed my face and arms, getting them as clean as I could.

"When we stop before sunrise for obvious reasons, I'll get us a hotel, and you can have an actual shower, but I hope to be closer to St. Louis by then," she said.

I tossed the rag back into her saddle bag and changed clothes. The jeans were a little long, so I cuffed them, fitting, as that'd sort of been the reason I was abducted in the first place.

This time, my grandfather wouldn't show up and shackle me. I had an aunt now, and she was a fucking vampire, something I tried hard not to think about.

"You mentioned St. Louis. Is that where you live?" I asked.

Becky laughed. It was a deep, rich chuckle that shook the belly and spread a grin to all who heard it.

"No. Goodness, no. We have a long ride ahead of us, Vedalia. I'm taking you to Maine, putting this entire nightmare behind you as best I can. You ever seen the ocean before?"

I shook my head.

"I've never left Arkansas. And my friends call me Val. I guess since you rescued me you can too," I said, smiling.

"Okay, Val. You've never left Arkansas? That changes tonight. C'mon, bub. Put your helmet on," she said, handing me a black flip-up helmet with a clear face shield. "You like Bowie?"

Shrugging, I said, "Sure. I've seen Labyrinth."

Becky raised an eyebrow.

"No, I mean, his music. Do you like his music?"

"Bowie makes music?" I asked, frowning. I knew he sang in the movie, but that was about the extent of my knowledge.

My aunt looked like she had been shot. . . again.

"Put your helmet on. I'll start up 'Hunky Dory.' I see any attempts your mom made to teach you about good music went all stove up to hell."

I smiled and put the helmet on. Becky started her bike, pulled out her phone, selected a playlist that began with a song called "Changes," and we rode off into the night.

My arms were snug around Becky's waist, and I remarked that for a vampire on a blood diet, she had a large pair of hips and an ass that could sink the Titanic. But I kept my grip solid, as though my rescue might be a dream that would fade if I didn't hold tight enough, and I'd wake up screaming chained to the radiator again.

As we rode north and crossed the state line near Branson, my brain started to accept the fact that this might just be real after all.

CHAPTER 2

It was strange being around people again. At 3 a.m., the Waffle Hut in Springfield was surprisingly half full. Most of the customers around us smelled of vodka or cheap whiskey. And I mean, stuff so cheap you could use it to run your tractor when diesel prices got too high.

Students from Missouri University — Springfield were nursing hangovers from whatever parties they'd bowed out of before their peers.

I was trying to breathe slowly. The loneliness when chained in the church basement or the isolated cabin had been emotionally crippling, but to suddenly be thrown back into a normal setting with people who knew nothing about abductions and cults was. . . jarring.

"I can hear your heartbeat still running like a

jackrabbit, you know?" my aunt, the mysterious vampire whom I'd only just met, said.

Shrugging, I looked down at the menu again, a single page printed front and back with the laminate starting to peel.

"I'd forgotten how many ways you could serve hashbrowns," I said. "Do I want them with tomatoes? Onions? Peppers? Syrup? I might just explode from anticipation."

Becky smirked, but her gaze remained.

"You can bury that anxiety in sarcasm all you want, but the advantage of being a vampire is I'll always know when you're lying," she said.

I rolled my eyes.

"Fine, you got me. Force of habit carried over from a childhood of neglect. I guess your 'be calm' command is wearing off," I said. How long had it been? An hour or two maybe?

My aunt stared at her menu for a moment, rubbing her chin, and said, "Yeah, you're my blood, so you have some resistance to my mesmerism."

That last word sank into my mind as I looked up from my menu.

"Didn't they call it 'compulsion' on 'The Vampire Diaries'?" I asked.

Becky didn't look up. Her tone changed to something dryer than a desert.

"Yeah, but they also made the mistake of running it for eight seasons, so who will you go with? The show whose only redeeming quality was Bamon or the cool fun aunt who buys you waffles and breaks you out of cult dungeons?"

Damn, she's good at getting me to smile, I thought, giggling. *Where has she been all my life? I'd have loved to have an aunt growing up.*

Our server came over, and I asked him for three waffles, two orders of hashbrowns with peppers and onions, a bowl of fruit, and a cup of black coffee. Becky looked amused and impressed. Ampressed? Then she ordered twice that.

Double damn. I respect a lady who can eat, I thought, nodding.

My chest started to quake, and I felt a low hum building up in my core. Instinctively pulling my arms and legs in tight, I curled up in the booth. I think this was a bit much rushing back into public again, even 3 a.m. public.

"You want me to mesmerize you again, Val?" my aunt asked, putting our menus away and flashing me a look of concern. Wow. Rescued from my cult dungeon and caring attention from an adult? I needed to buy a lottery ticket tonight while my luck was still running hot.

I just nodded as Becky leaned across the table, crimson irises lining up perfectly with my gaze once more. Her pupils seemed to vibrate as she whispered, "You are calm."

Numbness ran across my brain for a good 30

seconds before my shoulders slumped. It was all the fun of a CBD gummy without the weird aftertaste that came from the health food store I frequented back in Eureka Springs.

Leaning back in my booth, stretching, and feeling docile, I yawned, suddenly feeling like a world's worth of weight waddled off my shoulders.

"Shit, Becky. That's better than Lorazepam. Can you get me a prescription for mesmerization for my next 50,000 panic attacks?"

She smiled as the server brought over our coffees.

"Any time you need it between the hours of 6 p.m. and 6 a.m., you just let me know," she said, stirring sugar into her coffee before taking a sip.

I thought about that statement and was reminded once again the woman sitting across from me was a vampire. A member of the undead. Did her heart beat? How often did she have to drink blood? I had so many questions.

That must've been apparent on my face because Becky downed half her coffee, clicked her tongue, and said, "Val, I'll never lie to you. I know you've had it tough. My goal is to take you to my home, slowly make it your home, and support you in any way I can."

There it was again. Sudden care from a parental figure, and I just didn't know how to handle it after 17 years of damn near neglect.

"Can I ask you a few questions?"

She flashed me her palms and said, "I'm an open book."

Behind us, three booths away, a girl a few years older than me sat up long enough to look around and see she wasn't where she expected to be at 3 a.m. on a Wednesday. And then she went back to sleep on top of her dry waffle.

The cooks and server paid her no mind, other than to check that she was still breathing and that no guys were being creepy around her. Which. . . they weren't. Because they were too stoned or hungover to try it.

"Why are you taking me to your home in Maine? Shouldn't you have driven me back to my parents?" I asked.

Becky sighed and slowly reached a hand across the table, leaving it palm-up for my own hand. She had bad news. Oh god. They were dead, weren't they?

I placed my fingers in her surprisingly warm touch and looked confusingly down at her skin.

"I'm warm when I feed. Helps me look more alive. Over the next few hours I'll get colder to the touch," she said.

Nodding, I waited for Becky to get back to my parents.

"Val, I'm really sorry. But I don't know where they are. I got a letter a week ago from my sister. It was a string of apologies. She explained what your grandfather had done, that cocksucker, and that she and your father were leaving. My sister didn't ask me to save you. She just said you'd been taken a while back and told me to do whatever I wanted with that information. Frankly, I'm mystified. Their house was empty when I showed up, and I spent the next several nights working my way across the Ozarks trying to find you."

I should have been more upset. I should have cried all over the table and overturned my cup of coffee. But, hey, I was calm, remember?

And after what I'd gone through, the days and weeks of sleep deprivation, theft of privacy, overt humiliation, and unending preaching, this. . . just didn't seem all that bad.

"Was there. . . I dunno, signs of a struggle or something? Did Ebeneazar hurt them?" I asked, still a hint of caring bleeding through. They weren't the best parents, but it's not like they physically abused me. I had food to eat and clean clothes to wear. And that. . . was about it.

The vampire sitting across from me happily took a refill of coffee from the server before answering.

"The entire house was empty, bub. I'm sorry. That place was spotless. There was a for-sale sign out front. Some hedge fund will probably buy the property and turn it into a short-term rental or something," Becky said, closing her hand around my fingers.

I stared outside while I processed everything she'd said. The house had been cleaned? Fuck, that meant all my stuff was gone. My hoodies. My toy frog collection. Even my "Percy Jackson" books.

The table was quiet until our food arrived. A man and woman who parked a motorcycle outside came in and sat a few booths away. They were talking about how sad it was their favorite sandwich shop was closing. Cucumberman's was apparently a staple in Springfield.

Becky lowered her voice as she started eating the first waffle. We'd ordered enough food between us to cover the entire table. My legs kicked underneath, occasionally hitting the metal rod that supported it.

"Why don't you eat something? You'll feel better. I always feel better when I eat," she said. "Or drink."

Her mouth curled upwards with a devilish grin, and I snorted, unable to stay all that bummed around her. I wasn't in the best mental place right now. But before me sat a forest of food, each bite taking six years off my life.

I ate a buttery waffle and made a pleased, yummy noise.

"Oh, fuck me that's good."

Becky nodded.

"The important thing I want you to know is that you're not alone. I promise. You're welcome to stay with me and my wife for as long as you want. We can enroll you in school up in Portland. And if you don't like it, you can go to college somewhere super far away, chart your own path."

I stopped eating, eyes widening.

"You have a wife?" I gasped.

Becky honest-to-god blushed.

"Have for a while now. Her name's Jazmine. I think you'll like her. She has a big garden, plays in a band, and — oh yeah, she's a witch."

My jaw dropped to the table. I'd been adopted by a lesbian paranormal power couple.

"How did you two meet?" I asked, suddenly captivated by my aunts, that, again, I'd just learned of a few hours ago.

Finishing her last waffle and chuckling, Becky asked, "Sitting across the table from an actual vampire, and you want to know how I met my bride?"

"Uh, yeah! Being gay is what got me thrown into Bible Jail. My last few weeks have been nothing but abominations, brimstone, fire from above, and pretty much all the disturbing parts of scripture, which. . . is most of scripture. Suddenly, I get the chance to talk about girls, which I'm a big fan of by the way, and you're surprised?"

Becky laughed even louder now. Outside, clouds were starting to cover the moon. The wind picked up.

"Oh, my sweet niece. We, uh, met several years ago. I was breaking into a blood bank where she volunteers. Wasn't too bright. Was just really hungry that night. I didn't do my due diligence in scouting. Jazmine took me down pretty quickly with a powerful spell, and right before incinerating me, paused long enough for me to compliment her blouse. . . and her eyes. . . and her name, once she shared it with me."

I snickered.

"Gay."

My aunt smiled and looked down at her potatoes as if they might be hiding a tiny movie screen to play back that memory under the cheese and onions.

The grill popped to our right as the cook tossed on several eggs and strips of bacon. I couldn't help my brain as it thought, *May all your bacon burn. . .*

I smelled the salted pork and asked the server for a plate of bacon when she walked by again. She smiled, walked over to the cook, and asked him to throw more on the flattop stove.

Under his spatula, the bacon crisped up nicely. He threw on pinches of salt, pepper, garlic, onion powder, and even a little cayenne pepper. Then, he peppered the eggs into oblivion.

As the eggs were nearly finished, the cook pulled out a plastic bowl of pre-made batter and poured it into one of the four waffle irons with a motion so rehearsed you'd think he'd been doing it for 40 years. Actually. . . given how the guy looked, he may well have been doing it for 40 years.

I watched steam rise from the waffle iron, and the smell of baking batter flew across the room to me. I finished my waffles and considered ordering another when my bacon arrived.

That fried pork didn't stand a chance. I destroyed it and then my potatoes before leaning back and sighing, content for the first time in a month. You'd have thought I was starved the way I ate tonight.

Oh yeah. . . I was, I thought.

"So. . . you flirted your way out of being reduced to ash. Aunt Becky, when we get to Portland, you're going to have to teach me your moves," I joked. The vampire scoffed as she finished her food and accepted another refill of coffee.

She watched as steam rose and lazily drifted over the mouth of her drink, and I started to calculate the bill, looking at all our food. It was the first time I'd thought of such a thing. We'd put away enough grub for four people tonight. I was too hungry earlier to consider the cost.

Becky seemed to notice me crunching numbers and waved her hand.

"Val, easy. I got it."

Then I realized two women were going to take me in, and even if I just stayed with them until college, that was a hefty expense. Dad had muttered more than once there was nothing more expensive than raising a teen girl.

I called him out for the sexist remark and got sent to my room for sassing him.

"Are. . . are you sure you and Jazmine want to take me in?" I asked, frowning. Even I was aware that I could be a pain in the ass now and again. It's part of my charm. But Mom and Dad had chosen to bring my smart-ass into the world. Becky and her wife might only be taking me in out of pity or some moral obligation they felt as distant family members.

My aunt gave me a gentle grin and offered me her hand again. I took it, unsure if this would become a regular habit.

"You're far from a burden on us, okay? Truth is, vampires are sterile, and we've always wanted a kid. Not that we'd expect you to think of us as your parents or anything. Just. . . we'd be overjoyed to have you take our spare bedroom," Becky said.

My heart fluttered a bit in response to that. Mom and Dad never really seemed to want me around, and here was a couple that wanted a kid but couldn't have one. Just another way it became evident to me that the universe was a pretty fucked up place.

"I — I can get a part-time job after school to help pay rent," I said. "I worked in a grocery store back in Eureka Springs. Actually, it was the only grocery store in town."

Becky shook her head.

"We'd rather you focus on school and trying to rebuild your life, Val. Trust me, we're good on cash. Jazmine's father was an industrial chemist and invented a solvent that. . . um. . . does something really important for big machines. I dunno, you'll have to ask your other aunt. I don't have a mind for science. The point is, that it made him a small fortune, which he was smart enough to turn into a big fortune. Each of his three kids went to the university of their choice and has a trust fund," Becky said.

I shook my head. This just kept getting better and better. Maybe I'd been too hard in judging the universe.

"So. . . you're a kept woman, and she volunteers. What do you do with all your eternity?"

With a cheeky grin, Becky snidely said, "I travel across the country and rescue girls from cults."

Ha ha, I thought, rolling my eyes.

"The point is. . . we'll get you new clothes, and school supplies, decorate your room however you want, and still have plenty of money to buy pizza every weekend. We want you to heal in a completely normal environment. Well — as normal an environment you can have while being raised by a gay vampire and her witchy wife."

I snickered.

Taking a deep breath and reminding myself I was

grateful for the calm spell I was under, I looked up at Becky.

"So. . . you'll use that mesmerizing ability any time I ask?"

"Sure. But, if you think you're going to be very reliant on it, we might want to get you with a therapist. Actually. . . we'll probably do that regardless after what you've been through. I know a doctor who would be perfect if you want me to call her sometime next week."

Therapy didn't sound too bad, actually. Who knows what horrible trauma I'd picked up from being held prisoner over the course of a month? Hell, I'd have a free sandwich on my punch card in a week or two.

"How often do you mesmerize people? Seems like a pretty sweet ability," I said.

"Without consent? Never. I consider it a moral imperative to keep that particular talent in check at all times."

Not long after she'd said that the man who'd brought his wife into the Waffle Hut walked over toward our table. I froze and looked up. He appeared to be 70 but was probably somewhere closer to 40 and just lived a hard life.

He got Becky's attention and cleared his throat, putting a hand on her shoulder, which left my eyes widening.

"Hey baby, my wife and I couldn't help but notice

you from across the restaurant. We were wondering if you'd like to ditch the kid and come back to our place. I've got plenty of Pink Floyd albums and enough baby oil to fill a slip-n-slide."

The vampire didn't so much as flinch. She just leaned into his face, made eye contact, and said, "You don't want to guilt your wife into another threesome she'll agree to just to appease you. You want to go home, eat her out, and then rub her feet for two hours."

I put both hands over my mouth and tried to stifle a giggle.

The man looked a little lethargic for a minute. Then he nodded, said, "That makes perfect sense," and calmly walked back over to his wife.

We watched them chat for a couple of minutes, and then they took their food to go and left.

Turning back to my aunt, who had finished yet another cup of coffee, I crossed my arms. With a big grin on my face, I asked, "Would the senator from Maine like to strike her previous statement and enter a new one into evidence for today's hearing?"

Becky cleared her throat, handing the server a debit card.

"Okay — that looked bad. But what I meant to say earlier is I. . . consider it a moral imperative to keep that particular talent in check most times. Jazmine, who is immune, by the way, scolds me if I do it too often."

I raised an eyebrow.

"How does she find out?"

"She asks, and I tell her. I won't lie to my wife, Val," she said, chuckling and leaving a couple of twenties as a tip.

We got back on Val's bike and rode northeast for a few more hours. The cow pastures, hills, and forests became a blur in the dark, and I closed my eyes thinking about the future that awaited me. Living near the ocean would be such a change, as would, you know, freedom in general. I might have teared up a few times in my helmet thinking about having a bedroom and a family member who gave a shit about me. She legitimately cared about, not just my physical well-being, but my happiness, and my contentedness. What would that be like? I could only imagine.

Near St. Louis, the first specs of morning light started to threaten us on the horizon. Well, threatened my aunt. I'd be fine. I was just tired as shit.

True to her word, Becky got us a hotel. The clerk looked a little mystified that we were checking into a room at 5 a.m. instead of out of one. But she gave us a couple of keycards nonetheless.

Our room was on the fifth floor. The carpet in the hallway was blue and smelled like most hotels did. . . as though the place had been freshly vacuumed. To our frustration, the key cards didn't seem to work, and neither of us wanted to go back downstairs.

My aunt looked down the hallway in either direction and said, "Hold on."

I nearly gasped as her body dissolved into a translucent mist, flattened itself to the floor, and slipped underneath the crack at the bottom of the door. In two seconds flat it was over, and Becky was holding the door open, looking pleased with herself.

"You are so fucking cool," I whispered.

"I know," she replied and shut the door behind me as I entered.

The windows overlooked downtown St. Louis in the distance.

I jumped on the bed and bounced around on my back, giggling. This was a mattress! A fucking complete bed with a comforter, sheets, five pillows, and — and I'd get to sleep here! Holy fuck, it was amazing.

I'd never cried over a hotel bed before, but my eyes threatened to here.

I showered quickly and turned up the water as hot as it'd go, sighing in relief as my legs buckled. Everything was great. Perfect. Amazing. Flawless as a Mortal Kombat victory.

Bunching my arms up together and shaking with excitement in the shower, I squee'd. I fucking squee'd. It was hard to remember if I'd ever been this happy before.

After brushing my hair, I collapsed on a bed. The first rays of sunlight were peaking over the horizon as I looked outside and then shut the curtains.

"Okay, listen, Val," Becky said. "When that sun is fully up, my body will be dead to the world until sunset, alright? Don't freak out. You won't be able to wake me for any reason. You can scream, stake me, shake me, slap me, or set me on fire. I won't so much as twitch until the sun sets."

I nodded.

That was when she pulled out a handgun from the back of her pants.

"I promise that I will always protect you, okay? But I can't do much during the daytime. So I'm going to place this Ruger Mark IV pistol in the side table drawer behind the unnecessary Bible just in case there's an emergency before I wake up. Do you know how to shoot?"

I nodded.

"Dad took me to the range a few times and taught me safety basics. I was in the hunting club at school, too. I can be responsible with that thing and recognize it's only to be used as a last resort," I said.

"Good girl," Becky said, lying flat on her back and yawning on the bed closest to the television.

She popped her neck left and right.

"I mean — what I meant to say is. . . I consider it a moral imperative to keep my gunslinging talent in check at all times," I said, hoping she was awake long enough to hear that.

Without opening her eyes, my aunt grinned, revealing one of her fangs.

"Don't make me mesmerize the smartass out of you, Val," she said before fading into Oblivion or Styx or wherever a vampire's soul went as the sun rose.

I checked the locks on the doors two more times, made sure the window was locked, pulled the curtains tight, and saw that I had a round in the chamber.

Satisfied that this was as safe as I was going to get, I let sleep take me, dreaming of the ocean and sandy beaches that I'd never walked on before. For the first time in a long time. . . the future looked good.

CHAPTER 3

The parking lot before us was almost empty, just two cars sitting by a small brick building, waiting for their underpaid employees to return and take them home. I took a deep breath, putting my helmet on Becky's motorcycle.

I got up and stretched my legs, eyeing the neon sign over in the parking lot's north corner. "Green Cross Blood Donation? Like. . . the charity people who show up and help after natural disasters and give people a place to stay when their houses burn down?" I asked.

Becky put her helmet on the bike.

"Yes, and the largest provider of blood to hospitals and clinics in the country. Each year they take in more than four million blood donations," Becky said.

I raised an eyebrow.

"Your aunts are. . . part of their biggest financial donor pool each year. So they send us packets with stats summing up the previous year every January," she explained.

That. . . sort of made sense. I guess if they were rich, this was as good a charity to donate to as any.

"So. . . what are we doing standing in the parking lot of this particular donor center at 3:32 a.m.?"

Becky just smiled.

"I gotta eat, bub. Fresh blood every other day, or I start to get hangry. Then I need more blood," Becky said, like this was some normal thing, as though she was on keto or paleo or vegan.

But it wasn't normal, not for me. I was still getting used to my aunt being undead.

Shaking my head, I said, "Wait, you're going to rob this place of blood that's supposed to be for sick people? What if you take all their blood, and tomorrow there's a major pileup along I-70 in Dayton? Thirty people injured, and suddenly there's no blood. What then?"

Becky held up two fingers.

"For starters, Ohio sucks. And any blood I can deprive them of, I'm happy to. Second, I only take a liter or two. They won't even miss it," Becky said.

I crossed my arms and frowned.

"Can't you just find a serial killer and drink their blood?"

My aunt grinned, and I wasn't sure why I was

having such a hard time with this. Vampires needed to drink blood. I'd read Bram Stoker's book and had watched, like, a billion movies. This was just the way things were.

But. . . I didn't want the person who rescued me to hurt people, not innocent people anyway. Ronald fucking deserved it for helping to keep me imprisoned for a month. But this blood was vital for people who got shot or were in a car crash. I. . . wasn't sure I was okay with my aunt stealing it.

My chest tightened, and I clenched my right fist.

She's been nothing but a godsend for me these last couple nights, and I need her to be. . . to be a hero, I thought. *A good person that'll love me and welcome me into their family. Someone who takes out their recycling and volunteers at the food bank once a month.*

My aunt sighed, but not with impatience. She'd been really good about answering all my questions and concerns in good faith. And it's not like Becky had lied about anything. This was just another case of her brutal honesty on display.

"How many serial killers do you personally know, Val?"

"Ummm. . . just one. I had a locker buddy in school who brought a peanut butter and mayonnaise sandwich for lunch every day. He was definitely a serial killer."

There was that husky laugh from my aunt again. I couldn't help but smile after hearing it.

"Okay, aside from him. How many do you know? And how many serial killers do you think are in the state of Indiana right this second? Not counting any folks from Ohio crossing the border."

Why does my aunt hate The Buckeye State? I thought.

But I had to admit defeat. I didn't know any serial killers, and I didn't know where to find them. I just shrugged.

"Exactly. Vampires present a moral problem, right? Because you want me, as your aunt, to be a good person. And in your mind, no upstanding person would steal resources from people who will need them in an emergency. So you start to rationalize. . . why not let me exclusively hunt serial killers?"

That all made sense to me.

"Except serial killers are a sliver of the population, peanut butter, and mayonnaise sandwich eaters aside. There are more of me out there than there are serial killers. And regular killers. The time it'd take for me to track down a murderer and prove their guilt beyond a reasonable doubt would be more than a full-time job. It's not something I could do in 48 hours when I'd need more blood."

"Well damn. Maybe it's not as easy as they make it look in the movies," I said, looking down at the bike again.

A set of headlights drove past us on the road, but

then we were alone again in the rural town of Richmond, Indiana.

My aunt motioned toward the blood bank with her head.

"It's actually pretty easy. I hit up the three blood banks outside of Portland all the time. You walk in, mesmerize the staff, take a bag or two from the cooler, and ride home with your combo meal."

I flinched.

Math was never my best subject, but that meant my aunt was stealing from blood banks for something like 180 nights a year. Holy shit that was a lot of blood.

But she could be out hunting people, I thought. *This is the route of least harm.*

"I gotta admit, I didn't think this would be such an obstacle for you," she said. "Not that you aren't entitled to your own opinions and morals."

Looking over at the bushes around the blood bank, I crossed my arms. Why was this bothering me so much?

But I didn't need to ask that question. I already knew. My grandfather was a monster. He chained an underage girl to a radiator for 30 days. I didn't want the woman I'd chosen to move in with to be a monster as well. My brain was too tired for this level of nuance. It just wanted things to be simple. Stealing was wrong, especially from charity. And kidnapping was wrong.

Of course, I didn't dare speak these thoughts aloud to my aunt, not because I feared any punishment or wrath. But because I didn't want to hurt her after all she'd done for me.

"I keep forgetting you were on the debate team, Val," she said, suddenly. "Your mother mentioned in her last letter that your team won the state championship. So, of course, you're taking time to look at this from so many angles. Not to mention the fact that a vampire is involved."

When I looked at the chipped pavement and faded yellow parking lines beneath me, she seemed to know what was going through my mind.

Her tone softened, and she ran a finger over the handlebars of her bike.

"I won't ask you to come in with me. But this is something I need to survive. This afternoon, you ate a hamburger. A cow was raised and killed to make that food. For me, this is no different. I paid for that beef with a credit card on our hotel receipt. And I'll pay for this blood at the end of the year when we cut a check to the Green Cross."

I didn't know what to say to that analysis. It was certainly the point of view she'd lived with for. . . however many decades Becky had been undead. But I was still alive. Until two nights ago, I didn't even know vampires were real. They were all Alucard and Lestat, creatures made to fill the mind with fascinations of immortality and tragedy.

"Can you live with me knowing this is what I do? Because if the answer is no, and that's perfectly fine, we can try to find you a foster family or someone else to take you in. I'll respect that," Becky said, a sadness in her eyes that made my heart feel like a sponge squeezed and mashed to get all the water out.

She really loves me, I thought. *My aunt has spent the last 17 Christmases wanting to meet me, and now that we're on the way to her home, she's prepared to give me up. . . all for the sake of my comfort.*

That didn't sound like a monster to me. Blood stealing aside, this sounded like family, good people. So how could I judge her for doing what she had to in order to survive?

While my brain ran over the facts again and again, preparing logical arguments based on ethical stances and philosophical traditions that would make Chidi smile, Becky turned to walk into the blood bank.

My body moved on its own, following her. When I jogged up beside her, Becky smiled but didn't say anything. If she'd asked me then and there whether I wanted to go back to her bike, I probably would've faltered.

But I was determined to show Becky I'd stick by her side. This was the only way I could think of to do that.

She already knew I thought her a monster. I'd

given her a look I'm sure hundreds of people had throughout my aunt's life. The difference was, that I'd take action to show her I didn't care. I didn't care that she was a vampire, and I was just a high school girl tagging along for her dark deeds.

As we walked across the parking lot, Becky sighed again and put a hand around my shoulder, pulling me tight.

"I'm a monster, Val. But through the years, I've known decent monsters and horrific people. Rotten holy men, werewolves who live by a code. You can be on one side of the human spectrum or the other. But if you make a choice, you have to live with it. Good vamp, bad vamp, that's up to me. Good human, bad human, that's up to you. I try to be good, but my existence comes with a price. All magic does, as you'll see when you meet your other aunt."

I turned to look Becky in her crimson eyes.

"What do you mean all magic comes with a price?" I asked.

Behind us, another motorcycle drove by, and then the road was quiet again.

"All monsters are magic in some way or another," she said. "Magic keeps me from aging and gives me a handful of abilities. But there are prices I pay for my eternity, bub. I have to drink human blood, and I can never get a tan, not without a wicked sunburn anyway."

I wanted to smile at that, but my mind was still processing this lesson on magic.

"I steal blood to drink instead of hunting people like so many of my kind do. But I'm still taking from charity. So I try to balance that with good deeds elsewhere, spending some of my limitless time and accumulated wealth to better the world's grand karmic scale. Does that make me good? I dunno. The universe will have to judge that one day, I suppose."

Saying nothing, I continued to walk by Becky's side as silence fell between us. I could only hope she understood my lack of response was due to fierce internal debate, rather than hating or fearing her.

In the end, stealing blood from the Green Cross was as simple as Becky said it'd be. She knocked on the door, told security staff her bike broke down, and mesmerized them into letting her in.

Becky didn't hurt a single hair on their heads, just giving commands that they carried out without question. When she had a couple bags of blood, my aunt downed them, licked her lips that'd been stained red, and turned to leave, ordering staff to erase the security cameras for tonight and forget we'd ever been here.

We were walking back outside toward her bike a mere 10 minutes later.

It was like hitting a drive-thru. But that's when things took a turn. I wasn't sure where he came from, but a man stood before us and produced a bright silver light that hurt my eyes.

Becky hissed and recoiled, throwing her hands up as her skin started to smoke. Her eyes blackened, and the vampire crouched to the ground.

I looked at the light's source, and when my eyes adjusted, I recognized a silver cross, blazed in white fire.

A man wearing leather gloves and fatigues held the cross forward. His hair was buzzed, and he wore a camouflage vest packed with guns, knives, vials of liquid, and even a pocket bible.

One of his eyes was glass, and he scowled, looking over my aunt.

"Bold of you to hit this place twice, vamp," he said. "I thought you'd be smart enough to avoid coming back here, but it seems my gamble paid off."

Becky still covered her eyes and hissed, "Hunter, huh? Red Card or Gray Card?"

He didn't smile. The man appeared to be in his 50s. He was clean-shaven and in great shape. I assumed from my aunt's use of the word "hunter," he hunted monsters. Though I didn't know what Red Card or Gray Card meant.

"You trying to figure out if I'm gonna let you go?" he asked.

"If you've been watching me, I think my actions make it clear I don't kill people for blood," Becky said, gritting her teeth, fangs protruding as she seethed in pain from the holy relic.

The man spat onto the concrete.

"Gray Card would probably let you go for that. But I don't care who you hurt. You're a fucking monster, an aberration that doesn't belong in this world. And that's all the justification I need to stake you," the man said, eyes narrowing.

Everything about this hunter screamed ex-military. To him, this situation was black and white, with no room for nuance or debate. And as my heart pounded, he extended a hand to me.

"Come with me," he said. "I'll take you back to your family. You don't have to be afraid of her anymore."

"She's my niece, hunter. I am her family," Becky said.

"You're a vamp. The only family you have are other bloodsuckers. But rest assured, I'll find more of them to send with you to the other side."

What options did I have here? I doubted I could overpower this man. He had the drop on us and stood 20 feet away. There was no reasoning with him. I could explain for hours that Becky had saved me from a cult, and my mother and father were nowhere to be found.

I wanted to go with her, dammit. She represented a future where I might have everything I wanted. Family. A home where I wasn't neglected. Parents who actually took an interest in my life. I needed those things like Becky needed blood.

So, I made a decision, one I knew would change the course of my life forever.

"Come to me now, girl," the hunter said. "She can't move so long as I have her trapped with blessed silver. I promise you'll be safe."

My aunt shrunk a little more into the concrete as if she wished it would swallow her. The gray smoke wafting off her flesh was much thicker now, and I watched Becky writhe in pain. It was pain she'd rescued me from just two nights ago.

The hunter took a couple of steps toward us, maybe figuring I was frozen in place by fear and needed to be pulled aside.

I reached behind me and waited for him to get even closer.

Becky hissed louder with the next few steps this man took, flinching in greater agony. Her eyes were bloodshot.

When the hunter was about five feet away, I pulled out the firearm my aunt gave me for protection when she was asleep during the day. There was no debate here, no thought process, just primal action.

This man was hurting my family. I didn't stop to ask if he was a good person. I didn't debate the ethics of removing someone who hunted monsters, some of whom were probably evil. I needed my future with Becky and her wife, and he was taking that from me.

So I shot him. He seemed surprised by this. I watched him stumble backward with a look of pained astonishment. His eyes snapped wide, and I could only imagine what thoughts raced through his head. Probably something about how the girl he was trying to rescue shot him. A sickening gargle rattled from his throat followed by a distressed moan.

Next thing I knew, the hunter was lying there on his back, writhing as my aunt had been. The man dropped his cross, and the scorching light snuffed out as it left his hand. It clattered to the ground on the cement, echoing across the parking lot.

I fired three more times until he stopped moving.

And then I sank to my knees and let the cold horror of what I'd just done wash over me. Becky wasted no time taking the firearm and wrapping her arms around me. Even with the cross disarmed, she still smelled like smoke.

"You didn't have to do that," she said. "You could have gone with him. I would have understood."

I shook my head slowly.

"No, Aunt Becky. I want that future you promised me, a senior year with two parents and a loving home by the sea. I want to dream about college and know my aunts will care about every decision I make."

She held me tighter, my face pressed into her leather jacket.

"So I decided to become a monster like you. I killed him because he was hurting you," I said, shaking uncontrollably. Was I still blinking? I couldn't tell.

"Oh, sweetie," Becky said, pulling away so she could look me in the eyes.

"I can't. . . stop shaking," I said. "But I know what I did was right. Or maybe — I just know that I'd do it again. It's hard for me to think straight and tell the difference between the two right now."

Becky ran her thumb under my eyes to catch a few tears.

"Make it stop," I said, my lungs feeling like they were being squeezed. If they were coal, and this continued, my lungs would turn into diamonds.

"I'm tired of hurting. I just want the good part to start," I said.

Shaking her head and wiping away a few more tears, I watched my aunt's pupils start to pulse again. Her voice cut through my whimpering.

"You did what you had to do. You made a choice, and you're prepared to accept the consequences. But for now, in this moment, you feel at ease, understanding that you saved my life. You feel guilt, but it doesn't overtake you. You are resolute in your decision to become a monster and live with other monsters. And not one ounce of doubt remains."

With a sigh and drooping head, I asked Becky to take me home.

She nodded, picked me up, and put me on the back of her bike. I'm not sure what happened after I placed my helmet on. I assumed she dealt with the body and the staff who might have heard the gunshots.

But eventually, we left, and I fell asleep against her back, too numb and tired to stay awake. The shift from days to nights and all that accompanied it had drained me, as I'm sure she drained the hunter so as not to waste any blood.

Becky's words from earlier echoed in my slumber.

"You can be on one side of the human spectrum or the other. But if you make a choice, you have to live with it," she'd said.

I didn't know what would come of it, but I would live with this decision. I wanted a future. I wanted a loving family. And I wanted Aunt Becky to remain a part of my life for as long as I lived it, monster or otherwise.

CHAPTER 4

$\mathcal{I}$ still couldn't believe my eyes. We were standing on the side of a highway, cars driving by an hour before sunrise just outside a town called Wells. I'd spotted the sign that said "Vacationland" and had a slogan underneath that said, "The Way Life Should Be."

And it was the way my life would be from now on. Because this was going to be my home. Lobsters, blueberries, lighthouses, and Stephen King. What a way to spend my senior year.

But what really blew my mind stood before me with people walking in and out every few minutes. Becky came out and zipped up her leather jacket, smiling. I smelled a flowery scent from the foam soap she'd probably used in the bathroom.

"Less than an hour from your own home, and you couldn't hold it one second longer, huh?" I chided her to keep my brain from thinking about Indiana.

"Hey, watch it, Val. With or without a bladder the size of a silver dollar, I'm still an immortal who could chuck you into the ocean from here. You live by a coastline now, and I won't hesitate to use it," she said, ruffling my hair.

I rolled my eyes and went back to staring at the building in front of us.

"Really easy to impress, aren't you?" the vampire said, crossing her arms.

"I just can't believe your rest areas have all this. It's a building with a fucking gas station, clean bathrooms, a Burger Queen, and Sunken Donuts! Down south our rest areas are having a good day if there's toilet paper."

Becky snorted.

"Are you going to pee, or what? We're burning moonlight."

Realizing my aunt had a diurnal deadline, I darted across the parking lot and into the building. I returned with donuts in one hand and a breakfast sandwich in the other.

"Seriously? You went to both?" Becky asked, raising an eyebrow.

I shrugged.

"Why not? I didn't want to let this opportunity go to waste."

After scarfing down my food at a speed that

made even my bloodsucking aunt squirm, we hopped back on the bike and finished the last leg of the journey with purple and pink hues coming up over the ocean's horizon. Pretty sure I saw Becky flinch as we exited the turnpike and turned toward Maine's biggest city.

My head kept swiveling back and forth as we crossed the Fore River on the I-295 bridge. It was perfect timing because a massive airplane flew over-head, taking off from the jetport nearby. My mouth dropped as I watched the wheels fold into the plane. For a moment, I almost thought I could scrape my fingers along the bottom just by standing up on the bike.

I spotted a massive hospital along the shoreline ahead of us, the red lights along its roof blinking in the approaching dawn. I also noticed another bridge just east of us with more cars driving from Portland to South Portland and vice versa.

We rode the interstate a little further and got off exit six, coming alongside a massive park and green space called Deering Oaks. While Becky and I stopped at a red light, I noticed a large pond with a tiny island in the middle. A regal dollhouse stood on the island surrounded by birds swimming this way and that.

"For the geese," Becky yelled over the noise of her bike. "And during the winter when that pond freezes, lots of people come to ice skate on it."

Ice skating sounded both fun and terrifying. I'd nearly broken a knee just rollerblading around Eureka Springs. It was enough stress for Dad to finally confiscate my skates and get me a bike, which I managed to avoid wrecking. . . most of the time.

But I also had a soft spot for ice skating. It was the only Olympic event I watched every few years, and I also grew up watching the Charlie Brown Christmas special every December. They made ice skating look so fun and easy. . . at least until Snoopy tangled everyone in Linus' blanket and sent the gang flying every which way.

I think. . . I want to try it, I thought. *I wonder how long until the water freezes. November? December?*

As I stared at the pond, Becky, seeming to sense my thoughts, hollered, "If you want, we can get you some skates. There's an indoor ice rink with public skating times almost every day. Jazmine would probably be happy to take you."

I smiled. Dare I say. . . I was looking forward to something and having something to look forward to made it easy to keep my mind from thinking about it. I could think about skates and whether you wear a jacket on the ice. Jazmine would probably laugh as I fell on my ass at least once every lap I made around the rink.

Yeah. . . I'll just keep daydreaming about this, I thought. *No need to focus on any other things my mind keeps trying to revisit.*

Becky raced up a hill and turned left onto Congress Street. We passed a place called Longfellow Square, which had a large statue of someone sitting in a chair. Windows we passed were covered in posters for different musicians coming to town. Dawn grew closer as if chasing us from every direction. I felt my aunt straining with every red light we caught.

Too bad being a vampire doesn't come with traffic signal magic, I thought, clutching her hips a little tighter as we passed the Stateside Theatre.

Portland was coming to life as people walked to their favorite bagel or coffee shops, went to work, and opened their stores. It was autumn, and that meant cruise ships were docking almost every day, according to Becky. She'd rolled her eyes telling me about the tourists who packed the Old Port.

"It's a nightmare, bub. And you're just better off staying downtown or heading over to Woodfords to eat instead," Becky had said last we stopped.

We passed a Moonbucks, an art museum, and even a TV station in the heart of downtown.

"I don't watch them much anymore since they got rid of my favorite meteorologist. She actually left to become a high school science teacher," Becky yelled at the next red light.

Our journey continued northeast past a department store called Remy's. Not long after, I spotted several queer students with brightly-colored hair and pride flag pins on their backpacks crowding around the entrance to an art college.

"That kind of looks like a fun place to go to school," I muttered, my eyes following an androgynous individual with purple curly hair and a denim jacket. They were carrying a giant sketchpad and walked inside after scanning their ID badge against a receiver on the brick wall.

Oh, they're cute, I thought. *And that gives me another thing to daydream about. More ammo for my — shit. No, I mean, not ammo. Because I'm not thinking about the gun I used the other night.*

I flinched, and Becky turned her head to look at me. Then I squeezed my eyes shut and tried to force a different daydream.

Maybe. . . I can get a job as a barista nearby. And the purple-haired student comes in to order an iced coffee. I get their name. We could start chatting about their new sketches and — my thoughts were interrupted by a pickup truck blaring its horn at a cyclist running a red light.

Becky shook her head, and we took off again.

At the center of downtown towered a large monument of a woman overlooking the square. Beneath her feet stood a group of soldiers and the words "TO HER SONS WHO DIED FOR THE UNION."

Restaurants lined one side of the square, while a public library filled the opposite side. A large brick pathway was packed with demonstrators for. . . something. I couldn't read the sign as we drove by too fast.

More demonstrators rallied outside of city hall and gathered on the front steps. Their signs were also a blur, but they were angry. That much was clear as they chanted and shook fists in the air.

Sunlight crawled closer across the sky. We flew by a place called Lincoln Park, and I didn't even have time to smirk and sing, "It starts with one thing — " because Becky gunned the engine through another light.

Things raced by in a blur: another highway cutting through the middle of the peninsula, a drug store, and a cemetery. Then we braked coming into a residential part of the city called Munjoy Hill.

Becky pointed out a structure that looked like a lighthouse but was actually an observatory. A few restaurants popped up on either side of the street. But the neighborhood was also filled with old houses and some condos I didn't even want to know the price of.

My aunt swung right onto Atlantic Street and took us into a more packed neighborhood. No businesses here, just older apartments and homes. She parallel-parked and pushed me toward the front door with more vampiric strength than I expected.

"You can get your bags in a minute. Let's just go go go," Becky said, steering me over a brick sidewalk and toward a small two-story house with stone steps.

The bottom story was painted a faded blue with wooden panels on all sides of the building, while the upper story had white siding on some parts and gray shingles on others. In fact, the upper level may have been a half story as part of it was a slanted rooftop. What did I know? I wasn't an architect.

A side yard attached to the house was surrounded by a chain-link fence. A small flagpole stood centered in the mix of wild grasses, a rainbow flag waving below the Maine state flag.

"Huh, a pine tree under a single star. I kind of like that," was all I had time to mutter before Becky opened a door and shoved me inside a house that smelled of hazelnuts and cinnamon.

I stood there awkwardly as Becky patted me twice on the head, shut the front door, kissed a woman wearing a gray bathrobe in the middle of the living room, and then darted around the corner yelling, "Sorry, babe. Jazmine, meet Vedalia. Vedalia, meet Jazmine, my beautiful wife. Goodnight. See you in 12 hours."

In the silence that followed, I heard a body falling onto what sounded like a bed.

Holy shit. We cut it close, I thought, blinking and adjusting to the dim light of the room.

A few scented candles provided light as every window was covered with thick navy curtains. I turned to the Black woman standing before me, her hair dyed amber and styled into shoulder-length locs.

We stared at each other for an awkward moment as I cleared my throat. I know sunrise didn't leave my aunt with a lot of options for introductions, but this was chaotic. Or maybe I was chaotic. Jazmine stared in my direction with warm brown eyes before extending a hand toward me.

"Uh. . . hi. Like Becky said. . . I'm Val, her niece apparently."

Jazmine smiled and motioned with her open hand for me to step toward her. So I did, walking between a loveseat and a recliner onto a golden rug. My legs were stiff, and it felt like I was moving on stilts.

Becky's wife waited patiently. I gingerly extended my hand toward the silent homeowner. She gently took my wrist with one hand. With the other, she ran two fingers from my palm down to my veins. Then, she pressed down and closed her eyes.

I was at a loss for words, entirely unfamiliar with this greeting. I remained still and waited for her to finish. . . whatever she was doing.

Jazmine stood there holding my wrist and focussing on something. I had no clue what. But she frowned, and I felt my pulse quicken. That didn't seem good. A few seconds later, I watched her frown give way to an expression of sadness. Was she about to cry?

Shit, what did I do? I thought, my breaths becoming shallow.

At last, Jazmine opened her eyes, and she let go of my wrist, placing her hands on both sides of my face. We were about the same height, so she looked right into my eyes. And I saw. . . sympathy?

"I'm not sure what's happening, but if I upset you, I'm sorry," I said, hoping against hope I wasn't about to lose the new home my aunt had promised me.

Jazmine shook her head gently and then shocked me by kissing my forehead and pulling me into an embrace.

"Oh! Uh, it's nice to meet you, Jazmine. I uh. . . Becky has talked about you almost the entire way here," I said, my arms still at my sides.

I didn't expect this kind of warm greeting from my newest aunt, one whom I'd never met before. But she just held me there, not saying a word.

"I'm not sure what Becky has told you about me. I was kidnapped by my grandfather and imprisoned by his cult. We don't know where my parents are and — feel free to stop me at any time. I know she's been texting you, and I don't want to stumble through anything you already know."

She said nothing, merely keeping her arms locked around me.

My brain started to drift back toward Indiana again.

Fuck. Stop it, I thought, shaking my head. But Jazmine held me firm, her head on my shoulder.

"I mean — some stuff happened on the road. I'm sure Becky told you about that, though," I muttered, feeling my throat tightening.

Jazmine didn't flinch.

Scenes I'd pushed down into that funny little lockbox in my chest started to leak out, despite the chains I'd wrapped it in and locks I'd slapped over the container.

The deafening gunshot. The body hitting the ground. The light of a blazing cross fading into night.

No. Stay back, I thought. *She's gonna find out, and then I won't be able to live here.*

But the images and sounds just kept leaking from that chained-up little box in my chest like water. Silly me. I forgot to waterproof the trauma vault.

Rookie mistake, Vedalia, I thought, my chest feeling like it was full of gravel. My lungs barely had room to inflate. I couldn't breathe.

"I'm uh, not really sure what — " I started, choking back a sob. Goddammit, this wasn't going well. I threw up every wall I had to keep that shit locked down, and they were all cracking faster than the Hoover Dam in an action movie.

The final straw was what I'd said to Becky playing back in my head.

"I decided to become a monster like you. I killed him because he was hurting you," I'd said back in that parking lot. Right after I'd pulled the trigger. The trigger that killed a man.

Then and there, I lost all control. No box, no chains, no walls could hold it back anymore, and I threw my arms around this perfect stranger who'd been holding me for the last couple of minutes and bawled.

Any mesmerization had long worn off, and the pain coursed through my heart like a swollen river washing away its banks.

No words, just sobs, and gasps for breath. Did Jazmine know this was coming? Was this why my new aunt greeted me as she had?

I buried my head in her shoulder and started to shake as if my body couldn't cry hard enough to get everything out.

That's what I get for locking this away over the past couple of days with vampire hypnotism, I thought.

And yet, Becky had to know this was coming. We were only putting little bandages on my psyche. Just trying to hold my emotions together until we got home.

I'd been handed off to the living aunt like a baton while Becky rushed toward her dead sleep brought on each day with the sun.

But Jazmine didn't seem to mind in the least. Why? Why would anyone be cool with their wife bringing home an emotionally damaged kid with little to no warning? Surely pity wasn't this powerful of a force.

Then I remembered what Becky had told me back at Waffle Hut.

"You're far from a burden on us, okay? Truth is, vampires are sterile, and we've always wanted a kid. Not that we'd expect you to think of us as your parents or anything. Just. . . we'd be overjoyed to have you take our spare bedroom."

I guess crying was something kids did, right? We were afforded that right because growing up in a broken world was hard. It was doubly challenging when your grandfather led a cult and shackled you to a radiator for an entire month. And being forced to kill a man to protect your aunt? Shit. At that point, crying might not be enough.

I wasn't sure how long I sobbed. Jazmine was surprisingly patient, patting my back and holding me without wavering.

"I'm sorry. I didn't mean to emotionally puke on you without warning," I muttered, finally pulling back and wiping my face on my shirt.

Jazmine gave me a gentle smile, and I suddenly felt embarrassment climbing up my cheeks.

"Um, don't take this the wrong way. But I've been

doing all the talking so far and. . .," my voice trailed off.

My aunt made a fist with her right hand and brought her fingers to her lips, pressing them together for a moment, knuckles facing me.

I didn't understand, and then it clicked.

"Oh, shit! I'm so sorry. I didn't know you used sign language. Somehow Becky forgot to mention that on our road trip. Have you heard anything I've said?"

Jazmine nodded.

"Okay, so you can hear me just fine?"

She nodded again and once more pressed her fist to her lips.

I thought for another second and felt like an idiot.

"You're mute," I said, pointing to my throat. Wait, was that insensitive? I put my fingers down, and Jazmine just smiled and nodded.

She motioned for me to follow her, and my aunt led me into a kitchen furnished with stainless steel appliances and an island in the middle. Magnets in the shapes of different states covered her fridge.

My aunt motioned for me to sit on a stool at the island, which could comfortably seat about four people. It was painted blue on all sides, just like the walls of the kitchen. Coffee mugs with different lighthouses and boats painted on them hung from wooden hooks above the countertops.

Jazmine filled an electric kettle with water and set out two mugs. She opened a cabinet filled with tea and motioned for me to pick one. I chose a peppermint tea, and Jazmine picked the same.

The electric kettle shook a little as water bubbled inside, and after a few seconds, the plastic switch on the back finally clicked off.

My aunt filled each mug with steaming water, and we let our tea steep while she fetched a notepad and pen.

On it, she wrote, "Becky tries to treat my disability like it's no big deal. So, she doesn't tell people about it, preferring to let them figure it out when meeting me."

I nodded.

We sat in silence and without writing for a few minutes. Jazmine went to make sure the bedroom door was closed and then opened the curtains in the kitchen. Morning light came pouring through the blinds and brought a new energy to the room.

"Again. . . I apologize for emotionally dumping on you like that, Aunt Jazmine. That wasn't fair," I said.

She shook her head.

Jazmine crossed both of her wrists over her chest. Then she swooped them out in opposite directions in the shape of a "W."

"I'm really sorry. I will learn ASL. Hopefully, my

high school here will offer it as a language course when I start, but if not, I promise I'll find a tutor."

That brought another smile to my aunt's face. She wrote, "Safe." And then, "You are safe."

I felt a little less like crying now.

Jazmine took out her phone and turned it on, revealing a picture of Becky, washing her bike outside, soap suds dripping from the handlebars.

My aunt placed her phone on the table, leaving the picture on, and then wrote, "You saved her life."

I stared down at my tea, steam still drifting up from the mug lazily toward my face and vanishing before getting anywhere close. After crying into Jazmine's bathrobe like that, I wished I could disappear in a puff of steam. I didn't even know this woman, but she'd welcomed me into her home and let me cry on her. Who does that?

Family, I thought. *Your family does that. At least, your new family does.*

Jazmine tapped the countertop to get my attention.

I looked up, and on the pad, she'd written, "I know someone who can help."

Pulling out my phone, I searched for a video real quick. After watching it a few times, I put it back in my pocket.

Curling my fingers and bringing my hands together over my chest, I stuck my thumbs up. Then I rotated my left wrist back and forth, pointing my thumb toward me, then away, and back again, over and over. I'd hoped I was signing "How?"

My aunt tightened up my sign a little bit and then nodded. She walked over to a large brown purse on the counter next to a microwave. Digging around for a minute, Jazmine finally seemed to find what she was looking for and brought over a business card.

"Amandine Dubois, supernatural counseling," I read, raising an eyebrow. "I wouldn't turn down therapy. But don't you think I should see a —" I cut myself off, almost saying the word "normal."

So, I thought for a minute. And I tried again, quieter.

"Don't you think I should see a more. . . typical psychologist?"

Jazmine smirked.

"And tell them, what? That you killed a monster hunter to save your vampire aunt?" she wrote on the pad, underlining the words "hunter" and "vampire."

I flinched. She was right, of course.

My aunt held up both hands and made a gesture as though she was clutching a rope. I later learned that meant "Trust."

Yeah. . . okay. She could definitely be afforded some trust after letting me cry into her shoulder and welcoming me into her home.

One could be forgiven for thinking I was a bit short on trust after being held captive for a month.

But after Becky saved me, I figured the least I could do was give her wife the benefit of the doubt.

"Okay, Aunt Jazmine. I trust you. I'll go talk to Amandine."

She ran a couple of fingers down my cheek and then picked up her phone, sending off a text. We drank our tea, and I burned my tongue. Big surprise. But it was good.

Jazmine's phone was face down, and her camera flash blinked a couple of times. She flipped it over and texted back. This went on for a few more minutes until she wrote on the pad, "She can see you tomorrow if you're okay with that."

I just nodded and thanked her.

Wow, a therapist who specializes in monster trauma, I thought. *That ought to be an interesting experience.*

We sat there finishing our tea in silence when I turned to Jazmine and opened my mouth to form a question I hoped wouldn't come with regret. She smirked, and I would have bet money there and then she knew what I was going to ask.

"So... Becky tells me you're a witch?"

I phrased it like a question, hoping I could just vaguely hint at wanting more info, and she'd run with it.

She was merciful and nodded.

I felt like, generally speaking, most folks knew the basics of vampires. They were strong. They drank blood. Etc. But witches. . . that was a whole new ballgame. I mean, did they stir potions in big black cauldrons? Did they read your fortune? Did they write spells in grimoires to shape the magical forces of this world? The possibilities were endless. And I didn't have a clue what to ask Jazmine.

She seemed to sense this and wrote, "I'm an ink witch."

Furrowing my brow, I opened my mouth to ask something and immediately closed it, feeling too dumb to probe further into the matter.

When I didn't ask anything else, Jazmine lifted the right sleeve on her robe to reveal a beautiful tattoo of an orange, white, and black tiger spread from just below her shoulder down past her elbow. Its color was bright and looked like she'd just had the artwork touched up.

And yet. . . I was willing to bet Jazmine had worn this tattoo for years if not decades.

"Wow! That's amazing work, Aunt Jazmine. I've never seen a tattoo that looked so vibrant, almost like the animal was fixing to leap off your arm," I said, sticking my face a few inches closer for a better look.

Her grin widened.

She flattened her left hand and placed her palm over the tiger's head, blocking it from view. Jazmine took a deep breath and closed her eyes. Above us, the kitchen lights started to flicker, and her lips spoke a silent language that not even the most sensitive ears could hear.

The hairs on my arm stood as goosebumps paraded below my elbow.

"Aunt Jazmine?" I asked, raising an eyebrow.

She ignored me and continued working her magic. When she opened her eyes, I gasped as they glowed with an ancient golden power. Slowly, her fingers trailed down the full length of the tattoo, and everywhere they touched, the image faded, vanishing from my sight. This continued until her arm was blank. . . as if needle and ink had never touched it.

I stared at her umber skin where a tiger had previously stalked.

"Where did it go?" I whispered.

As my aunt's eyes returned to normal, she pointed behind me. I spun and, to my horror, found a Bengal tiger staring up at me with yellow eyes. The ferocious predator was easily 10 feet long and weighed a couple hundred pounds.

I fell backward toward my aunt, ass hitting the floor and pain shooting down my legs. The tiger slowly walked toward me, as if bored.

"Okay, you made your point, Aunt Jazmine. Great trick. Very lifelike illusion. I will never question the power of an ink witch again," I all but whimpered, backing against her leg.

My aunt grinned and looked down at me with

the pad, on which, she'd flipped to the second page and written, "Her name is Cymera, and she's very real."

Right as I spun back to face the approaching tiger, heart racing like a goddamn Nascar driver, the animal proved her right, placing a gigantic murder mitten on my belly. I felt its weight press lightly upon my guts as, again, I whimpered. Cymera slowly extended her claws, and I watched the flaxen nails slide out so effortlessly between her digits and onto my shirt.

It was almost as if Cymera was asking, "Do you think they're fake now?"

In my head, I heard Smaug yell, "And do. You. Now?!"

"Truly, oh great Cymera, you are the greatest of calamities," I whispered. And, as if in amusement, the tiger retracted her claws, pulled her paw back, and then headbutted my shoulder, knocking me down flat. Though I suspect the gesture translated to, "I'm not going to kill you. . . today."

"You bring your tattoos to life?" I asked, looking up at Jazmine. She was upside down from my point of view on the gray tile floor.

She wrote something on the pad and held it down for me to read.

"That's. . . upside down, Aunt Jazmine. Er — I guess I am."

The witch flipped it over, and I read, "Or maybe they were already alive when they became my tattoos."

That silenced me quickly. As the rest of her arms and legs were covered by a fuzzy bathrobe, I couldn't see what other magnificent creatures my aunt might have tattooed on her body.

"Fair point, Aunt Jazmine. You. . . are an ink witch and very powerful. I will never sass you or give you any of that attitude we teens are so famous for."

My aunt gave me a silent chuckle before writing, "Would you like to see your room, my humbled niece?"

I nodded as Cymera gently chewed on my leg to illustrate how big her teeth were. And it turns out the exact measure of her fangs was "pretty fucking large."

Mercifully, with prodding from my aunt, the Bengal tiger let me up. My pants leg was now covered in tiger slobber. But as I'd just promised not to sass Aunt Jazmine, I stifled a cough and followed her upstairs.

She let me walk in first. My feet landed on a soft gray carpet. The first thing to catch my eye was my closet. The sliding doors were giant mirrors with knobs where the glass ended and the wood began.

A queen-sized bed with a comforter covered in

colorful fish sat to my right. A nightstand carrying a seashell lamp stood next to it.

The walls were painted a dark shade of blue, and large photos of lighthouses and docked boats covered the space between my windows. The ceiling slanted downward from the doorway to the floor across from me, following the shape of the roof.

A short, wide dresser with starfish and silver dollars for the nobs stood near the closet, and blackout curtains hung over each window to block out sunlight.

The bedroom had such a retro feel to it, and I adored every inch.

Jazmine held up the pad where she'd written, "We can redecorate whenever you want."

I shook my head.

"It's perfect, Aunt Jazmine. I love it as is. In fact. . . it feels really peaceful."

I stuttered with those last words as a deep exhaustion overtook me. The adrenaline of seeing a giant tiger was wearing off, and traveling for days on the back of a motorcycle across the country was finally catching up with me.

My ass planted itself on the bed without permission, and I felt my eyes droop.

Traitors, I thought, yawning and stretching.

"Is it okay if I crash for a bit? Sorry to cry and sleep. I'm sure I make a great first impression," I said, sighing.

Aunt Jazmine walked over, kissed me on the cheek, and motioned for me to lie down. She tore a new piece of paper off and wrote, "Welcome home, Vedalia" before handing it to me.

I slid off my pants and shirt, climbing under the covers.

Holy shit. What's the thread count on these? A thousand? I thought, feeling dragged into slumber even faster. *I'm sleeping on a goddamn cloud.*

My eyes snapped open when I felt a massive tiger paw her way onto my bed, placing two murder mittens on my belly and curling up around me.

"Um. . . down?" I dared with a whisper. Cymera's tail flicked over the light switch and plunged the room into darkness.

I flashed my aunt a pleading look. She remained at the door, bathed in light from downstairs.

Jazmine once again crossed both of her wrists over her chest. Then she swooped them out in opposite directions in the shape of a "W."

I recalled that was the sign for "safe."

Hey, look at me, I'm learning, I thought. *Fine, tiger nap today. Monster trauma therapist tomorrow. I think I'm going to like my new life here.*

Cymera chuffed, pushing me back down with a massive paw and maybe five percent of her strength. I would come to learn later that big cats aren't capable of purring (except for cheetahs, but they cheat the rules). So. . . tigers chuff instead of purr.

As Cymera chuffed two or three more times, and I closed my eyes, I amended my most recent thought.

I think I'm going to like my new life here. . . AND my aunts.

CHAPTER 5

Well, here I was. Monster therapy. When I sat in that basement considering all the possibilities for my future, visiting a counselor with experience helping everything from ghosts to zombies wasn't on my scorecard.

Her office was. . .cozier than I imagined. Was that the right word? I guess cozy was as good a choice as any to describe everything from the scented candles to the chairs that were so comfy I risked falling asleep and taking a nap if I sat in them unattended for too long.

Gray curtains hung next to a large window overlooking a little inlet I discovered was called the Back Bay. That was also the name of a neighborhood here in Portland. Jazmine and I had spent the morning walking the trail around it, smelling salt air, passing by more middle-aged moms walking their dogs than I could count, and generally getting in some good exercise before she treated me to bagels and coffee.

Now Jazmine was two rooms away in a little waiting area reading a Neil Gaiman novel I'd already forgotten the title of. It was really long, though.

My eyes glanced over at a tiny fountain by the door. It featured a sandy beach with plenty of mermaids lounging about, discussing what I assumed were current events.

I rolled my eyes at the unintentional pun.

C'mon, Val. I thought. *Humor as a defense mechanism only works if the jokes are actually good.*

The wooden door next to the fountain was old and had a frosted window in the top half of its structure. Written on the glass were the words, "Dr. Amandine Dubois, Counseling for the Emotionally Curious."

I sank more into the cozy red chair and closed my eyes for a moment. Two moments. Three moments. It didn't help that the back of the chair was covered in a fuzzy blanket. And without thinking, I unfolded it and draped the fabric across my legs.

Sighing, I sank more into the chair and mumbled, "Shit. I've accidentally sentenced myself to a nap."

My sleep schedule was still all kinds of fucked after traveling at night and sleeping during the day. Now, sitting in this office at 3 p.m., I wasn't sure if I was supposed to be getting ready for bed or just waking up.

The door opened slowly, and I bolted awake, trying to look like I'd just been glancing around the room, the same as when Dr. Dubois left. Why did she leave again?

I was suddenly reminded when the smell of hot chocolate floated across the room toward me.

"Sorry. I — "

"Made yourself at home," the extraordinarily French woman giggled. "That is good. It's what I want. You need to know this is a safe place to discuss any thoughts or feelings that plague you."

My new therapist wore black slacks and a cream sweater. Her black hair was tied in a braid that hung over her right shoulder. The cream sweater matched her skin, which was covered in freckles. The therapist's almond eyes looked over me with an aura of patience as she handed me my cocoa. It was then I realized one of her eyes was made of glass.

"You go all out, don't you?" I muttered, taking a drink and letting out a slight moan at how good this was. "Holy shit! Where did you get this? I know it didn't come out of a package."

Dr. Dubois sat down in her chair and crossed her legs, long black boots shining in the sunlight pouring through the window.

"I suppose you're right. I import this cocoa by the tin from Switzerland. It's one of the few things I refused to leave behind when I came to your country," she said. "Good chocolate, that is."

"How long have you been here?" I asked.

"Long enough to know that your cheese, your wine, and your chocolate cannot be trusted," she said, taking another sip of her drink.

Nodding, I sipped my hot chocolate.

Silence filled the room, but it wasn't uncomfortable. Thanks to the chair and chocolate, I was extraordinarily relaxed.

I finally asked, "So. . . how does this work? You talk first? I talk first?"

My therapist grinned into her mug.

"I love those movies. If for no other reason than I get to look at Oscar Isaac. That is one handsome man. I don't care if he's being rescued by Natalie Portman or piloting a ship. I would watch him do it again and again."

Grinning, I sneered and took another drink.

She's very personable, I thought. *And she looks to be right around his age. I bet they'd make a great pair.*

"But, you can talk whenever you're ready. You can ask me questions. I'll tell you no lies. Whatever you need to know to feel comfortable opening up to me," she said, reversing her crossed legs.

Outside the window, a flock of seagulls flew by, making all kinds of racket. They were the loudest birds I'd heard in my short 17 years. But I did adore the fact that they signified I now had a new life.

Maybe. . . I should start with the old life. Keep things simple. Go in chronological order.

"Perhaps I can just start at the beginning? When this whole mess began a month ago?"

Dr. Dubois motioned for me to start wherever I felt ready.

"Okay. . . I don't have all the facts yet. I only knew a month ago I'd just come out to my parents. Told them I'd been asked out by this cute girl at school named Mika. And they kind of ignored it. Like — I wasn't scolded as I expected. They just. . . didn't talk to me about it."

My therapist set her mug on a side table and folded her hands in her lap, listening.

"I remember telling Mom how Mika and I liked the same music and had a lot of the same classes at school. I couldn't remember being this excited about anything. And since she wasn't yelling at me, and instead going through the motions like usual, I figured that was a good sign. They were going to let me date her and just ignore that I was gay like they ignored my debate team meetings or my field trip permission slips."

Then, my mind took a turn, and all the hot chocolate in the world couldn't stop the ship from running aground on jagged rocks.

"That night, I heard Dad talking on the phone with Ebeneazar, his father. But the conversation didn't sound angry or heated. I didn't think anything of it. That is. . . until I awoke handcuffed to a bunch of copper pipes in my grandfather's church basement. I thought I'd been kidnapped by a serial killer. Nope. It was just my religious nutjob of a papa."

His face appeared in my mind. That fucker. Ebenezer was a large man. Looked like he could wrestle a grizzly bear and come out on top. I always thought he looked like a countrified version of President Snow. Big old belt buckle. Fluffy white hair cut nice and neat. Brown boots that clicked with every step he took. Nice jeans. You wouldn't suspect him of kidnapping a girl. Sending soup back at a restaurant, maybe. But not abduction.

My fists clenched on the mug as I pictured him that first day in my newfound captivity.

"Vedalia? Are you okay?" my therapist asked.

I nodded.

"Sorry. Just replaying that first day in cuffs. You see, I expected him to yell. I expected him to backhand me. I expected. . . all manner of physical abuse. And what I got was so much worse. He just explained, in a way that seemed to make total sense at the time, that I'd scorned the grace of God. It wasn't necessarily my fault. This is an evil world after all. I was just giving in to temptation. But he was going to fix me, Dr. Dubois."

She kept her hands folded and remained still as a statue while it started to rain in my heart, the wind picking up. These were signs of a storm building.

Until now, this shit had been in a vault. I hadn't even told Aunt Becky.

Clutching my mug tighter and ignoring the burn against my fingers, I sighed.

"Ebeneazar had this way of talking to you like he could just make sense of anything. It was a loose authority you didn't need to fight back against because, hey, he's not screaming. He's not even frowning. The old man was just explaining a problem, and this particular problem happened to have my homosexuality at its core. But my grandfather promised me he'd make me normal, Dr. Dubois."

There was that word again. Normal. The fuck did that even mean? You weren't causing trouble in society? You didn't stand out too much when people's eyes scanned the streets looking for people and things out of place?

Normal was marrying a linebacker on the high school football team at 18 in your parent's backyard and popping out a baby before your age started with a "2." Kissing girls didn't fall into that category. It didn't come anywhere close. And he explained that, day after day. All the answers were in his worn, black Bible with faded gold lettering on the outside.

"You can just call me Amandine if you like. Amanda also works if that's too hard to pronounce," she said, gently.

"Thirty days I sat with a steel bracelet digging into my wrist. That jagged metal biting into my skin was the only thing keeping me company. Well, that and the wall it was attached to. Some days, I'd get so lonely down there, tucked away from the sun, that I was almost grateful when Ebeneazar came down for a little devotional. You ever felt that? Grateful to the person hurting you?"

Amandine nodded.

"Believe it or not, I have felt that gratitude. It's like a sweetened little vial of poison. Goes down smooth enough, and you don't even realize something's wrong until your heart is racing 1,000 miles a minute, and you're foaming at the mouth."

I stood from my chair. We'd hit a new level of bonding when I found out this monster therapist was in the same league of fucked up as me. And that excited me because there was no holding back now. She could handle anything I said or revealed.

"The last few mornings, I expected to wake up with my wrist bound again. I expected my aunts to just be a delirious dream I made up to cope with all the trauma. And CLOMP CLOMP CLOMP, I'd hear his boots coming down the wooden stairs again. Another attempt to deconstruct everything I am so he could feel righteous in the eyes of his god. It was a war of attrition for him, but for me, it was just another day in the meat locker, swinging back and forth on my hook wondering if today would be the day I agreed to surrender everything just to get out of that fucking room.

"Five minutes in the sun, two minutes, thirty seconds would be enough of a treat to make me take a free dive into the baptism pit of his little country club/cult."

Amandine's eyes widened now, and she nodded.

"We've punched the emotional core," she said, reaching into her pocket and pulling out a stone disc the size of a coaster. Its polished black surface glowed with a curious orange light as runes and sigils on both sides came to life.

My eyes widened, too.

"You're a witch like Jazmine?" I asked, not really in fear, but in confusion. My aunt hadn't mentioned Amandine to be a practitioner of magic.

Amandine nodded.

"In a way. Whereas your aunt is an ink witch, I'm an empath. I deal in the manipulation of your heart's energies and all the subconscious nooks and crannies where your trauma likes to hide itself. I've been waiting for our connection to grow strong enough that I could help you, and it appears we're just about there."

The therapist's hair started to rise as her eyes glowed orange, and her magic stirred like a snake unwinding after hiding coiled beneath a pile of leaves. The empath whipped her hand, wrist popping loud enough for me to flinch. And the disc spun into the center of the room, orange sparks flying in all directions.

I felt her magic climbing into me, like a kitten crawling up your leg with its little claws. Nothing about this presence felt threatening. Rather, the energy waited patiently on the porch of my soul, seeking permission to enter. I kind of appreciated that in an odd way.

"Vedalia, I know you've been hurting. Jazmine said your trauma was dire. I see now she was right. Do you trust me to take some of your pain away?"

"Will it hurt?" I asked, pulling back a little bit.

But my therapist shook her head.

"It'll feel like emotional sinus pressure. Then your nasal cavity clears, and you can breathe for the first time in days," she said.

Wow, a neti pot for the soul, I thought. *That's kind of handy.*

Did I trust Amandine? Well, I trusted Jazmine. And Jazmine trusted the empath, so that was good enough, right? Plus, she brought me bomb-ass hot chocolate. An untrustworthy person would have given me something from a dollar store packet. The kind of shit where the powder doesn't dissolve no matter how hard or fast you stir, and all you get is a warm mug of poo water.

I nodded, and my therapist stretched her hand toward the stone disc. It spun faster and faster. A spectral hand made of Amandine's magic floated up from the disc's center. And darkness filled the room.

No sunlight from the window was enough to keep this shroud away.

My therapist stood and walked to the disc, placing her hand inside the spectral fingers like a glove of her own energy. Then she approached me and placed that glowing hand over my heart.

I flinched, expecting a shocking sensation or a frigid grasp. Neither came. And when I closed my eyes, I could almost hear a symphony playing in the back of my mind. Something grand, powerful, and magnificent. My shoulders slumped, and I let Amandine's magic all the way into my heart.

"One final question, Vedalia. And remember that I'm right here beside you. You're not alone in facing this harsh truth. Tell me, what's the worst thing Ebeneazar did to you, the thing that gnaws at your ribs, that makes your mind scream, that makes you wish you could set the world on fire?"

Shit. I wasn't crying anymore. This wasn't sadness. It was just blind rage. And I shouted, "He took away my fucking control!"

I couldn't leave. I couldn't talk to my friends. I couldn't even decide what or when to eat.

"When Ebeneazar wanted to talk, he did. And I didn't have the choice to stop listening. I couldn't tune him out. He could come and go whenever he pleased, and I'm horrified my grandfather might just show up one day to do it all over again. You want to know the worst thing Ebeneazar did to me, Amandine? He robbed me of the ability to feel in control of my life like my choices could be snatched away at a moment's notice, and I won't have the power to fight back."

With my last burst of rage, fear, and loathing, the empath grimaced and pulled her spectral hand away from my heart. As she did so, I felt something snag in my chest. And I flinched. She pulled harder, and I let Amandine have whatever she'd found rattling around in my chest.

She came away with a tight glowing ball of green light. Her fingers clasped it with all their power. Once it cleared my chest, the empath ripped her hand from the spectral fingers, and the energy attaching them to that stone disc popped like water in hot grease.

Then, the spectral hand was yanked back into the stone disc like a retracting tape measure. It snapped into the magic item and vanished from sight. I watched as the stone slowed, the sigils dimmed, and the magic faded from Amandine's grasp. Once it came to a complete stop, the disc fell to the brown carpet below and didn't move again.

Slowly, I remembered how to blink.

"How do you feel?" Amandine asked, still standing beside me.

At that point, my lungs reminded me they needed air, and I took it in by the gulp.

"I feel like. . . I can breathe," I muttered, surprised

at how much less doom seemed to fill my subconscious. Someone had opened a window and let all the smokey air out.

Without warning, I hugged Amandine. And she giggled, patting me on the back.

"Damn. You really pulled all that grief out of me. I feel amazing! Like I want to go run a marathon," I said, bouncing on the balls of my feet. "Well, okay, maybe not a marathon. But mentally, I could run a 5k or something."

The therapist smiled and retrieved her stone.

"I didn't take all your grief. Just a chunk of it. Think of it like emotional surgery. I just cut out a chunk of bad tissue," she said, putting the disc in her pocket.

Raising an eyebrow, I asked, "What will you do with that?"

"The same thing I do with all the others, Vedalia. Toss it into the sea and let Mother Nature cleanse it at her own pace," she said, walking over to a calendar on her desk. "But you feel good?"

I nodded.

"Good enough to return to school? Jazmine tells me she's ready to enroll you whenever you're ready."

"Hell yeah. A month trapped underground even made me miss AP Calculus. Let's do it," I said.

With another laugh, my therapist lifted her calendar, looking ahead to the following week.

"How about we meet again next Tuesday?"

"Sign me up for that, too," I said. "Thank you so much. I really can't put into words how much lighter I feel after that."

My therapist picked up her cocoa and finished it all.

"My pleasure," she said, returning the empty mug to its coaster. "Now. . . about feeling powerless. Let me remind you that your grandfather has no idea you're in Maine. You have two aunts who can and will kill to protect you. And. . . you don't have to feel powerless if you don't want to."

Cocking my head to the side, I asked, "What do you mean?"

Amandine just grinned and said, "Ask your Aunt Becky. I imagine she'll have a rather. . . creative solution to your problem."

azmine and I parallel-parked in front of my new home. I looked over the blue house and felt a stir of calm stretch out in my chest like a lazy cat waking up from its nap to go get dinner.

This was my home now. I didn't have to worry about being hurt here, not when a fucking tiger could leap off my aunt's arm and run down the hallway to kill my attacker. And certainly not when a member of the living dead could appear as mist behind any invader and tear their throat open.

Here. . . I felt protected. But I wanted another coffee. And that was probably elsewhere, a place I might not feel as safe. The sun was getting lower, and I checked my phone. It was just after 4 p.m.

"Shit. Does it get dark this early every day?" I asked.

My aunt smiled and pulled out her phone as she typed something. She showed me her notes app and written in small font were the words, "Daylight Savings Time."

Shrugging, I said, "Well, I guess that means Aunt Becky wakes up sooner, right?"

Jazmine smiled and turned to face their bedroom window, which was covered by blackout curtains. She blew a kiss to her slumbering bride.

"I think I want to go grab another coffee if that's okay," I said, rubbing my arms against the afternoon's autumn chill. This was my new home, but I was a Southern girl at heart. And that meant being in humid hellfire for nine months of the year. The other months, it rained. And maybe you'd see a snow flurry that fled faster than an absentee father seeing a pregnancy test. I was used to the heat. The cold? I wasn't even sure I wore a winter coat at home for more than one week out of the year.

Here? I wanted a coat to walk down the road and get coffee in November.

As I rubbed my arms for the third time, Jazmine went inside and returned with an old pink L.L. Dean coat. It had more pockets than the vest of an ex-Russian assassin. But the inside had a layer of wool that wrapped around my body. The outside consisted of Nylon and at least two zippers. I wasn't sure what the second one did.

But it was warm.

Jazmine opened her maps app and showed me a convenience store around the corner on Congress Street called "Hilltop Bodega."

She then handed me $5 and started to walk inside. But I caught her wrist, feeling a little bit of fear quaking in my heart. My eyes searched the ground for anything to focus on.

"Your grandfather doesn't know you're in Maine," Amandine had said just an hour ago. And it's not like I had a phone with me to track. But still. . . even with that bit of trauma lifted from my heart by the empath, I hadn't regained any confidence in my ability to protect myself.

My aunt nodded as I put the money back in her hand. Then, she put her index and middle fingers together on each hand. Jazmine pointed them toward me and quickly shook them up and down. I would later learn that sign meant "Let's go."

With a sigh of relief, I let her lead me up the road toward Congress Street, one of the main thorough-fares through the peninsula.

I didn't expect Jazmine to scold me for being scared to leave her side. But I did anticipate a flash of annoyance or at least exhaustion. We had walked almost four miles this morning around the Back Bay trail, after all.

Munjoy Hill was no joke. It really was a large hill that came up from the sea and then descended toward downtown. I imagined it'd be fun to ride a bike down, but a pain in the ass to pedal up. Then again, coming from Eureka Springs, I was no stranger to hills. I spent the first 17 years of my life running here and there downtown, up and down hills between the school and mom-and-pop shops.

Hilltop Bodega looked like a triple-decker house with a convenience store on the first floor. Two ancient payphones sat to the right of the entrance, and I wondered if they still worked. The first story was painted green, and above it sat a level of gray and then a level with brown shingles and small windows peeking out over the neighborhood.

Huh, I've never seen a bodega before, I thought.

I came from a place where if you wanted food you went to a grocery store or a gas station. But this was like a combination of the two, minus the fuel pumps outside. It was right here on the sidewalk for anyone to walk in.

Jazmine and I passed a large ice machine going inside, and I wondered how many months of the year it actually sold bags of ice. Like. . . maybe two?

The bodega had a large sign on two sides of the building that said, "Coluccy's Homemade Italian sausage," accompanied by a red logo for America's most popular soda.

Inside the bodega, worn tile floors and shelves that probably hadn't been updated since the '80s greeted us, full of boxed and canned goods. A grill and fryer in the back told me they made food here, too. The whole place smelled of onion rings and sandwiches.

I was surprised to find an actual bodega cat lounging on a random counter by a front window. Fluffy brown and gray fur made the little rascal look about as big as a young tiger.

"So, you must be one of the Maine Coons I've seen so much of on Instapic. God, you're even bigger and fluffier than all the pictures I've seen put together."

A little purple collar around the cat's neck revealed her name to be LaDonna.

This particular cat seemed friendly enough, slowly slapping her tail against the countertop every few seconds. Her little pink nose snooted against my fingers before she decided I was friendly enough to pet her.

She had a purr loud enough to rattle the counter she rested on.

Fucking adorable, I thought, petting her for several minutes before realizing I'd come here for a coffee, and Jazmine was waiting on me. She was making small talk with a man behind the register.

"Oop, I gotta go LaDonna. But don't worry, I'm sure I'll be back here all the time to waste my aunts' money. Bye!"

Running back to the cooler, I reached inside and grabbed a glass bottle with a brown label that read "Moonbucks Frost Brew — French Vanilla."

Spinning to run up to the register, I almost ran into someone. With my reflexes out of control, I bumped into a shelf loaded with cans of salted peanuts, knocking a few tins to the floor with a loud clatter.

Flinching, I shut my eyes tight.

"You good?" a girl's voice asked as I slowly opened my eyes and looked up to see who I'd nearly run over.

I gasped.

"Purple Hair Girl!" I shouted, way, way louder than I needed to. In fact, these were words that shouldn't have been spoken at all. My stupid brain had failed to catch them before I made a fool of myself. That was, sadly, a regular habit in my life. I wished desperately for the tin cans of nuts to hide me.

This was the girl I'd seen walking into the art college carrying a massive sketchpad, one almost as tall as me. She stood in front of me with her arms crossed and an amused look on her face.

My eyes darted down to her black band t-shirt with a familiar singer plastered on the front and the words "My Chemical Courtship" written underneath in a script font. Her red skinny jeans outlined the curves of her thighs, but I immediately looked up, heat rising to my cheeks.

Nope, we're totally not checking out this stranger I

almost knocked over, I thought. *That would be creepy and rude.*

If I could help it, I'd like to avoid adding anything to my rudeness today, be it embarrassment, creepy, dorky, or any other adjective that would so perfectly describe my gaping jaw at this moment.

"Hey, Coffee Girl. You good? Or do you have any other nicknames for me I need to be aware of?" she asked with a voice that was. . . not necessarily mean. There was a chill to her tone, but it didn't sound like something she could help. And again, the grin on her face beneath those lovely amber eyes (*stop it*) said she was joking.

It was practically in jest, whatever the fuck that meant. That was a word people used they had a general idea of but not a precise definition. Those same people also tried to use the word "hence."

As my eyes darted over the lace top of her t-shirt, revealing a very pronounced collar bone and cream-colored skin, I tried to think of something witty to reply with. Her wavy purple hair captured my gaze again as I felt my cheeks somehow heating more.

"Oh no," she mocked. "What if that wasn't a nick-name? What if 'purple,' 'hair,' and 'girl' are the only three words you can say? I hope I'm not being insen-sitive," she said, her eyes catching the light in a way that made me do a double-take. Did they just do that thing animal eyes did in the dark when the light hit them? No, that'd be weird. Right? Then again. . . how normal was my life right now?

When I couldn't think of anything smart to say to the pretty girl, I blurted out, "You too. I mean — shit. Um, sorry have a nice day!"

Then I shuffled up to my aunt and hoped Purple Hair Girl would somehow develop 30 seconds' worth of amnesia in the next few moments.

I handed my coffee to the cashier, and he scanned the barcode. He was a tall and slender man with hair that'd turned gray pretty early in life.

Wow, now that's the epitome of a swimmer's body, I thought.

The man's brown polo shirt lined his toned form as he handed me my coffee.

"You must be Vedalia. Jazmine here was just telling me you've moved to Maine and will be starting school soon," the man said, with a quick blink that I could've sworn mirrored Purple Hair Girl's.

How are they doing that silver light thing? I thought, before clearing my throat and stumbling for words.

"Oh, yeah. I'm looking forward to seeing the school. I've been out for. . . um, about a month," I stuttered, trying not to tell the man I'd been held hostage for 30 days.

"Well, I'm sure you'll see my daughter there. She's a senior, too," the cashier said, motioning with his chin. My blood chilled, and I suddenly felt stiff as a statue.

With a Herculean effort, I managed to turn my head back to Purple Hair Girl. She flashed me an exaggerated dainty wave with a few fingers.

"Seems you've already met Agatha. I bet she'd love to show you around when you're enrolled," her father said.

I tried to swallow the lump in my throat. Twin voices in my head simultaneously screamed, "Fuck yes!" And "Hell no!"

Agatha's smirk only widened as she called out from across the store, "My friends call me Aggie." Her tone was that of a mock southern belle. I tried to frown. My accent wasn't that thick. But I didn't have the strength to do anything in her gaze except reply, "My friends call me Val."

Her head cocked to the side a little, automatically adding 25 percent more menace, and she said, "Great. I'll see you around. . . Val." Then she turned and walked through a door marked, "Employees only."

I watched her go, my jaw falling again.

Yup, I thought. *I'm so fucked.*

When we got back home, Jazmine checked the kitchen clock and discovered she was late for her band's rehearsal. I watched her throw a guitar case into her car and rush to leave. But not before signing something to me.

Jazmine held one hand flat, palm up. And with the other, she put her index finger to her lips. Then, she moved her index finger to her flat palm, pointing it straight at me and silently giggling.

I raised an eyebrow, but she just kissed me on the forehead and left with a big smile. I repeated the gesture later for Becky, and she laughed.

"She's teasing you, saying you have a crush on Agatha," my aunt said, making herself tea.

Heat returned to my cheeks as I stamped my foot and hissed, "That's bullshit! If anything, Agatha was rude. She made fun of me at the bodega."

Becky flashed me a knowing smile that could only mean one thing.

"You like Krabby Patties, don't you Squidward?" that look said.

I tried my best to ignore that and change the subject. All of a sudden, the room grew quiet. Or maybe that was just my nerves.

"So. . . I went to see Amandine today," I said, clearing my throat.

Becky nodded.

"Great. She's really helped me through the years. Do you feel alright?" she ventured, looking over at me with a cautious glance.

"Yeah, no — way better than I have in weeks. But. . . there's something else I need," I said, feeling my heart rattling like a jackhammer.

My aunt, the vampire with super sensitive hearing, seemed to sense this and cocked her head to the side, waiting for me to ask the dreaded question.

"Will you. . . turn me?" I somehow choked out.

Becky didn't scoff. She didn't sigh. She didn't get angry or shout. The vampire just continued to let her tea steep. And then, almost so quiet that I didn't hear her, my aunt whispered, "No."

My heart sank, and I felt like a doctor had just denied me a lifesaving operation. I wasn't mad, but I did shout a little. It was fear, I think. Nerves. Teen hormones. Some shit.

"B — but you have to!" I stammered. "Amandine said you would. That it was the only way for me to feel protected again."

Becky lifted the tea to her lips, and with the patience of eternity, slowly drifted her crimson eyes to mine. Oh shit. Was she about to mesmerize me? No, she wouldn't. That'd be a huge violation of my trust. And this vampire standing across the island from me is the one person I know would NEVER hurt me.

"You're 17, Val. Trust me when I say. . . you don't want to be a teenager for the rest of forever. It'd suck. Being a teenager for seven years is long enough. And, to be entirely honest, I'm not even sure most people would want to be stuck in their 20s forever. I think I was lucky enough to be frozen right at 39. But there are still times I wonder what being turned at 45 or 50 would've been like," she said.

I looked down at the table. She was right. I knew she was right. But I still felt scared, like she was taking away the only tool I'd ever get to protect myself.

"Look, you're about to enroll in high school, right? If I turned you, how would you finish your senior year? There's not exactly a night school around here where you can attend class with Yuki, Zero, and Kaname," she said.

I raised an eyebrow.

"Forget it. Before your time, I guess. Damn children," she muttered, sipping her tea.

I tried again to argue, but my heart clearly wasn't in it. I just felt lost and was clinging to the only idea I'd had all day to feel safe and secure.

"But Amandine said — " I was interrupted.

"Don't tell me what you wanted to hear the doctor say, my young niece. Tell me what she really said. And believe me, I know that's a hard skill for teens to learn," Becky said.

I crossed my arms.

I'll give you a hard skill to learn, I thought, pouting.

But that gave away as I sighed and thought back to exactly what the empath had told me at the end of our session.

"She said. . . I didn't have to feel defenseless if I

didn't want to. And then she suggested you'd have a creative solution to my — my fear."

The vampire walked slowly around the island and pulled me into a surprise hug. With one hand, she patted the back of my head.

"Oh, my young niece. Vampirism isn't a jacket that you can put on when you're cold and take off when you're too hot. It's a violent and magical change that rocks your body to its core, changing everything from your chemistry to your psychology. And the costs are many. You haven't seen me lose control to hunger. You haven't seen just how badly sunlight scorches my flesh, smelled the smoke that comes racing over the puss and blisters that form in seconds. I've surrendered so much of my body to this change, and it'll never be undone," she said.

She was still right. I knew she was. But hearing why I was wrong didn't make me any safer.

"I won't even consider turning you until you're at least 25. Watch me. Observe my life, my choices, my price. Take the next few years to really weigh if this is something you want to commit to. Because when you choose to don this cloak, there's no taking it off."

I pulled away and nodded, looking down at the floor.

"I understand what you're saying. But. . . I'm still scared, Aunt Becky. You want me to go to school day after day, heart quaking with each step, wondering if my grandfather might be around every corner?"

She grabbed my chin lightly.

"I do think I have a solution if you're interested."

Without hesitating, I nodded. If the solution was to wear a rubber chicken costume to school every day, I'd do it. Anything to feel safer. Though. . . I'm not sure how that would help me. Maybe anyone brave enough to wear that to high school for the entire year was so steadfast in their courage that fear didn't even penetrate their heart.

"So. . . vampires can select a human to lend a piece of their power. It's called establishing a First. You have access to a portion of my vampiric strength, my speed, my stamina, and perhaps even a little of my magic. I don't know. I've never done this before."

My eyes widened.

"But! There are costs even here, Val. You'll share a portion of my hunger, an annoyance at the sun, and drowsiness during the daylight hours. Sanctified silver will also be able to hurt you quite a bit," she said, crimson eyes drilling into my own.

I gulped, trying to process everything she'd just said. A portion of her power. Would that be enough to help me feel safe?

Wait. . . did she say her hunger? I thought.

With a nod, she seemed to sense my question.

"Yes, my hunger. Not for blood, per se. But you'll probably wind up craving meat like nobody's business. The need will rip your stomach apart with famine if you're not careful, and you'll be running into the cafeteria scarfing down the entire tray of sloppy joe mix just to satisfy it. Understand, Val. What I'm offering you is still dangerous. I'll be watching you like a hawk, and if you start having issues, I'll recall my power in an instant."

That seemed fair. So, I nodded.

"Do you still want to do this?"

I nodded again.

Becky smiled and took my hand, placing her other hand on my shoulder. Her grasp was tight, but it didn't hurt.

"I'm right here. You're going to feel cold for the first few hours as your body settles, Val. If at any point it gets to be too much, you let me know. I'll stop the process immediately."

Tightening my grip on her hand, I blinked and threw my eyes up to meet her gaze, committing to whatever this process entailed.

"Let 'er rip," I said with surprise gusto. Whatever was about to happen, it couldn't be worse than being chained underground for a month, right? Sure, I'd never be a vegan, but you know what? Fuck those guys. They were right up there with Crossfitters on my list of "Shut up, please."

Mist filled the floor around us, and I felt my aunt's fingers drop to sudden subzero temperatures. Her eyes widened as a bloody light glimmered and danced in Becky's irises. My aunt's power crept over the cabinets, the fridge, and then the stove before finding me.

I suddenly felt like I was falling into a chasm, but my feet were still planted firmly on the floor. Her grip steadied me. That is. . . until I saw a shadow, bigger than her own, emerge from behind Becky. I gasped.

"Look at me, bub," her voice called, and I dragged my eyes back to her own.

The living shadow took shape as a cloak, wafting through the kitchen, solidifying until it was thick enough to knock a few magnets off the fridge. When it raised for the third or fourth time, I watched that cloak dissolve into dozens of tiny shapes, squeaking noises filling the kitchen.

Unable to look at my aunt's eyes anymore, my jaw dropped as I spotted a swarm of bats flying through the living room, circling through a bedroom to pick up speed, and then rushing back into the kitchen as fast as their little wings would carry them.

Without warning, the shadowy bats slammed into me, and no matter how tight Becky's grip remained, I was lost to cold shadow. Everything went dark.

CHAPTER 7

My eyes flickered. Where was I? Everywhere. Nowhere. Deep inside the bounds of my psyche, perhaps.

But where I was, it wasn't far enough to get away from that voice. His voice. I heard it through the void.

"Granddaughter! Where have you been?"

His voice felt like the sound of grease dripping into a cooking fire, and my heart plunged as I spun. He's there. Ebeneazar. Just as plain as can be, western shirt and thick brown boots. Neat, puffy, white hair. I spotted his hands on his belt buckle.

"I've been looking for you these last few days, was afraid you got away from me," he said.

My chest heaved, and I stumbled backward.

"I did get away! You can't have me anymore," I hiss.

"Now, now. I know you're upset. But don't worry. We can fix this, and start over again. It's not too late. And this isn't your fault. You're the victim here," he said.

I shook my head. How was this happening? Here in a place with nothing I was being hit with everything. My legs felt heavy and stiff as a rusted gate. My eyes started to water. And a desert seemed to grow all at once on my tongue.

He's right, ironically. I am a victim. ... just not in the way he believes, I thought.

"Take my hand, granddaughter. You're down the road but not totally gone, certainly not a lost cause. I can sanctify you once more. And you can rejoin your family," he said, extending his fingers toward me.

I jerked backward, my throat seizing like it was caught in a giant's fingers, pulling in tight. And all at once, I wanted to scream, vomit, run, hide, and repeat it all in that order.

"Don't touch me," I shrieked, feeling the ground of whatever we stood on rising to meet me.

"The darkness has you, Vedalia. But I can free you. Just — come along now," he said, moving closer. For every inch I ceded, he advanced, gobbling up the space like a toddler mowing through a pack of animal crackers.

And then. . . my descent abruptly stopped. His fingers halted their drive as I felt a chilled grasp on my shoulder. The smell of leather and snow took my breath away as I glanced over to see a familiar set of crimson eyes.

"Aunt Becky!" I choked out as she wrapped an arm around me and spun me behind her. My face smooshed into the shoulder of her leather jacket, and I felt her arm bent around my waist behind her. The strength to toss a pickup truck like it was nothing held me in its grasp.

"You can't have her, old man. She's my niece, now. I'm protecting her," she said, baring her fangs.

Ebeneazar gasped, eyes widening. His fear — it's the first time I'd seen it. And it's here, just like mine.

"So. . . you're the monster that took my precious granddaughter away," he said. "I always wondered where Vilonia's blood was hiding. You were the rotten sister whose stench I occasionally smelled on my daughter-in-law. But I never saw you."

The vampire held me tighter.

"It doesn't matter who I was. Or who Vilonia was," she said.

My eyes widened. It was strange hearing my mom's name spoken between two people from opposite sides of the family.

"All that matters is who I am now. And in this moment, I am Val's aunt, her guardian. You won't take her from me, and I won't leave her ever again," she said.

I felt renewed swelling in my chest.

Someone cares about me, I thought. *I have a home where someone cares about me.*

Taking deeper breaths and feeling more relaxed, I lay my head against Becky's shoulder.

"You can't have her, you damned vampire. Her future is mine," Ebeneazar hissed. He didn't move forward, but his voice cracked like a whip against my ears. I slunk behind Becky. The movement was weak and pathetic, but I didn't want to see him or hear him anymore.

"Val's future is her own. It is the sum total of nothing less than her full will and choices. You do not get to rob any more time from this poor girl. I'll protect her from you or any other hell this broken world tries to unleash upon her."

My grandfather sneered, and I heard Becky whisper, "Didn't you say you were a monster now?"

I blinked. My words from Indiana came back to me.

"I decided to become a monster like you," I'd said after killing that hunter.

Looking up at my protector, I nodded.

"Then take the power from me you agreed to wield, and get out of here. I'll take care of this fool," she said, turning to kiss the top of my head. "Go on. Nightmare's almost over."

As if on cue, I felt darkness envelop me. I was suddenly cold again. Frigid. But I had to hold out. This was the choice I'd made. If Ebeneazar represented some bastardized version of the light, then I'd freely given myself to shadow. It was the better option 10 times out of 10 in my mind.

Ice spread from the floor of this void up my toes, ankles, knees, legs, and the rest of me. I bathed in the power of magic birthed from blood and held nothing back from it. This was trust. I believed with all my heart Becky would protect me. She'd sworn it. I'd seen her kill to set me free. And she'd kill again to keep me free. When the chill had swallowed up every last inch of me, the ice cracked and splintered.

Shards of my aunt's power shattered and flew everywhere, specks of shine dancing in the darkness.

Looking down, I saw my body covered in a crimson-red cloak that danced around me. It radiated power, but no warmth. This was darkness, not light, not fire. The power and speed of pure shade granted to me by the one person I trusted more than any other.

There'd be a price to pay, she'd said. And I'd pay it. But right now, I just needed to get up and go. With all this energy swirling inside me, I suddenly felt. . . invincible. My body vibrated with the possibilities and excitement. As I had before I woke up in Ebeneazar's dungeon of holiness. Back when I was just a normal girl who was thrilled about dating Mika. The world was still good and so full of potential. I was practically bulletproof. My only weakness was a pop quiz in AP Physical Science.

Now... I had more. So much more. My legs were tightened springs, coiled to the max, and ready to carry me in any direction. Horses, cheetahs, those little lizards that darted across the water, they all wished they could run this quickly.

I rocketed away from my grandfather, the exact opposite direction into the empty nothing as fast as my new abilities would carry me. The more power I used, the further my body temperature plummeted. But I didn't care. I just needed to be away. So fucking far away from that man.

And I soon would be.

"Don't you dare run from me, child!" was the last thing I heard Ebeneazar say as I raced through nothing back toward something.

I will run. So far that your horrific light will never reach me, I thought. *If that makes me a monster, then fuck it, I'm a monster.*

A blur. A dash. A zip. I was all these and more bursting across the empty space with superhuman speed. It felt good, great actually. The further I got, the lighter I became. And eventually, I felt my lungs inflating to their old size again.

"I can breathe," I whispered.

My aunt's words replayed over and over in my head.

"And in this moment, I am Val's aunt, her guardian. You won't take her from me. I won't leave her ever again."

She was my protector. With her power, I was stronger than ever before. And when my strength wasn't enough, hers would be. That was her promise.

Carry me into that better future, I thought. *One given to me freely by monsters when everything else was stripped from me.*

And then I crossed the finish line. There was no cheering or champagne. No crowd rushed to my side to jump up and down. I simply hit the end of that void and bolted awake.

A new girl possessed, I stood in the dark of my room and held my arms wide, feeling power coursing through me like I'd never felt before. With a deep scream, I announced to the world that I was finished being afraid. Done being a victim. This was the start of me clawing back a life and future for myself. And nobody, no shit-for-brains cult leader, was going to take it from me.

Bending forward to catch my breath, I felt a hand on my shoulder.

"There she is. Welcome back," Aunt Becky said.

I smiled and continued filling my lungs with air. Looking down, I saw a mix of blood and some kind of blue gel on my shirt. A pretty big gob of it, actually. Raising an eyebrow, I turned to my aunt.

She frowned.

"He poisoned you, Val. You coughed all that shit up just before bolting awake. I didn't know what to make of it until I realized your new abilities included quicker healing. My power in your body pushed out whatever he infected you with . . . pretty violently, too," she said.

That's why I was so prone to anxiety and panic attacks after we left, I thought. *It wasn't just the trauma. That shitass poisoned me!*

"I figure it was one last chain to keep you tethered to him. But you broke it," Aunt Becky said.

Turning to her with a slow smile, I said, "We broke it."

The vampire kissed the top of my head, and my phone revealed it was around midnight. Shit, I'd been out for a few hours.

"Hey Val," Becky said with a mischievous tone. "Wanna go test what your new powers can do?"

We stood on the shoreline of the Eastern Prom looking out over dark water and a few islands that dotted Portland's coast.

"So that's. . .Peaks?" I asked, pointing to an island. Becky nodded.

"Yup. It's mainly a summer thing. Even folks who have houses there typically only use them when it's warm. The island gets real empty as it gets colder," Becky said, checking the pockets of her leather jacket to find a tissue, two quarters, and a small chunk of quartz.

"But there are ferries that run out to the islands every day?" I asked, taking another whiff of salty air and low tide. It was still so foreign to me.

My aunt kneeled and brushed some sand off a flat orange rock. It fit neatly in her grasp as she blew more of the sand off.

"Mhhhmmm. They leave from the harbor, which is basically around the corner from here. See that trail over there?" she asked, pointing to a paved pathway that crossed the beach. "It wraps around the peninsula and leads back toward the marina and harbor. There's a dock where cruise ships come to town and ferries depart for the islands. Jazmine can take you when the sun's up. It's kind of fun to look at all the boats coming and going."

A yellow street light with an annoying hum illuminated part of the beach that we had to ourselves. I watched a few green crabs scurry for cover as I stepped into the light. A nearby parking lot was deserted. And why wouldn't it be at 2 a.m.?

Some of the bigger towns near my home, like Springfield and Fayetteville, had places that were open 24/7. Shopmart, the world's biggest grocery store chain, was headquartered nearby. And all the BiggerCenter Shopmarts were open day and night. A few restaurants were, too.

But here in Portland? Most businesses were closed around sundown. And what few bars and restaurants that stayed open later typically called it quits by midnight or 1 a.m.

Night owl wanting some food? Forget about it. I wasn't even sure there were convenience stores open overnight around here. This may have been the biggest city in Maine, but it was still a sleepy little town overnight.

Looking down at my shadow, I blinked and rubbed my eyes. Something didn't look right. The form was. . .misshapen? This did not look like the shadow of a 17-year-old girl.

Am I really that gangly? I thought.

"Something wrong, Val?" Becky asked, walking over.

"Uh. . .my shadow is broken. It's not rendering correctly. Maybe I need to update my video drivers?" I asked, chuckling nervously.

Becky looked down and then smirked.

"Oh — that. Yeah, it'll look normal to everyone else. But what you're seeing there is the curtain being pulled back a little. My power is wrapped tight around you like a cloak. And that's going to impact you in several ways. One of the smaller ways? Your shadow, which is what you see when light hits you, is a bit closer to that of a bat. Because you're a little closer to a bat now," she explained.

I just nodded and cocked my head to the side, looking at the shape a bit differently.

"Oh! I see now. Those are my shoulders, and behind them, those curved lines are kind of like wings. My fingers look a little longer, kind of like claws. And my head seems a bit more pointed," I said, letting my eyes adjust like one of those puzzles you had to look closely at before gradually zooming out to see the whole picture.

When I turned back to Becky, I noticed she was

gone. A bit of mist darted across the sand near my feet. Tiny squeaks filled my ears until I scanned the darkness to find the source. A fuzzy bat glided here and there on leathery wings over my head.

Holding out my hand, the little creature darted toward me and hung upside down from my fingers. Her upturned nose and tiny black eyes twitched, looking over my face. She folded her wings in and jiggled her ears until I giggled.

Then, just as quickly as she'd made the initial transformation, I watched my Aunt Becky let go of my fingers and fall toward the ground. In another rush of mist and cold air, her shape expanded into the more familiar vampire who'd rescued me.

She knelt for a moment before stretching and standing up.

"You didn't give me any warning before changing," I jokingly scolded her.

Becky tightened her leather coat and raised an eyebrow.

"How exactly am I supposed to warn you before I transform?" she asked.

"Easy," I said, spreading my arms wide. "You shout, 'Bat!' And then you change into the tiny, fuzzy bloodsucking creature of the night."

My aunt rolled her eyes.

"No, the rules are, you only have to do that in. . . *New* *York* *Citaayyyy*," she said, in her best imitation of Matt Berry.

I snickered.

"So. . . can I change into a bat?"

My aunt shrugged.

"Dunno. Like I said. You're the only person I've ever made a First. Some things I can guess. Others, I'll have no clue until they happen," she said. "Which is why we work on control and secrecy first."

Above us, a gull cried out loudly into the night and flew up the road back toward Munjoy Hill. I watched it for far longer than I thought I'd be able to. Eventually, it disappeared over the crest of the hill opposite the ocean.

"Some abilities will happen so subtly that you won't be aware of them until I point them out. For example, your night vision. You tracked my bat form in the darkness. And you watched that seagull far past the point a normal person would be able to."

Nodding, I held my hand up to my eyes and waved it slowly back and forth. Nothing seemed all that different up close. But when I focused in the distance, I could make out shells and sand dollars a hundred feet away. Individual waves that crested several feet from shore were clear to me. Even boats that were anchored further out appeared as though I were standing right next to them.

Pretty fucking sick, I thought, looking back at my hands.

"Other abilities, you'll discover with practice and

prodding. Let's test out that vampire strength and see how much you've been given," Aunt Becky said.

I struck a boxing pose with my arms up and said, "Oh, I see. An epic nighttime duel on the beach to test my strength. Bring it — " I was interrupted by Becky vanishing from my sight and sweeping my feet out from under me.

Without warning, I became well acquainted with the sand. It tasted about like I imagined it would. Crunchy. Lifting my face with a sour expression, I spit out a truly biblical number of grains. Taking a deep breath, I stood up and brushed myself off.

"Cheap shot. But now that I'm aware of your tricks, I bet — " I was once again interrupted and eating sand salad without any warning.

Becky's laughter from across the beach added further insult to injury. I spit out an entire sandcastle and stood up slower this time. Brushing sand out of my hair and remarking that I'd definitely need a shower when we got home, I sighed.

"No, my young niece. No duel. You won't be testing your strength against mine. We already know the result. You'll be testing your new strength, which I've yet to see any of, with these," she said, revealing that smooth stone in her hand.

She held that the entire time I ate sand, I thought.

"A rock?" I said, a little disappointed. "I figured we'd do something epic like. . . go to the gym and bench press 500 pounds. Or visit a train yard and play catch with a locomotive."

Becky shook her head.

"Not everything needs to be epic, Val. Especially when you're trying to stay off the radar. Do you know what happens when people see you using magical abilities that are physically impossible for most folks?"

I didn't respond.

"That's how you get hunters after you. Now, maybe you get a lucky draw, and it's a Grey Card Hunter. You talk them down. Show your humanity. And they go on their way. But the more likely outcome is you stumble into the crosshairs of a Red Card Hunter. I don't need to remind you how that went," she said.

My heart skipped a beat as I remembered Indiana. Looking down at the sand I'd so recently enjoyed swallowing, I let out a deep breath. She hadn't spoken with a scolding tone, but Becky made her point all the same.

"The powers I've given you aren't a blank check to show off, Val," she said, suddenly appearing in front of me. Becky placed a hand on each shoulder and looked into my eyes. "They're to help you stop feeling like a victim. So that if you need them, they'll be there. Be secure in your person and what you're capable of. That control is what separates responsible monsters like me and Jazmine from ones who simply give in to bloodlust and mad instinct. That's what we're learning here tonight."

Becky flipped my hand over and placed the stone in my palm. It didn't have a single bit of warmth to it, despite the vampire holding it for several minutes.

She's going to need to feed soon, I thought. *Becky doesn't have an ounce of heat to her right now.*

"You're a country gal. So I'm sure you've spent countless afternoons skipping rocks across ponds," Becky said, pointing to the ocean with her chin. "What's your record?"

I thought back to sneaking onto Mr. Bishop's cow pastures to skip rocks when I was bored back home. It was about a half-mile hike through the woods, but it was worth it to spend some quiet time alone where nobody could reach me.

"I guess. . . maybe six or seven skips? The ponds back home weren't all that big," I said, my eyes darting to the limitless ocean spread across the hori-zon, broken up by islands.

For a few seconds, we just stood there in the night wind, listening to the waves hitting the sand before fading to foam and washing back out. It was like the ocean was steadily reaching for us, each wave that hit the shore a hand spread wide to catch our toes.

Holding my right hand back, stone leveled between my fingers, I whipped it forward. Nothing about my motion or speed hinted that this would be a stronger throw than normal. But I watched that rock skip across the water like a jet crashing into the ocean at full speed. Tch. Tch. Tch. Tch. Tch. Tch. Tch. It skidded and bounced far further than I expected. I counted about 11 or 12 skips before it sank beneath the waves.

All at once, I felt exhilaration rocketing through my chest. Excitement like a kid finding a new toy under the Christmas tree. There was a spark, and all of a sudden, I wanted to launch another stone. Scanning the beach like a frantic old lady searching for just the right coupon at checkout, I felt Becky take my hand again, placing a slightly bigger rock in my grasp. This one was dark blue and had specs of white scattered over the surface. But it was still flat as a pancake.

"See? You weren't even trying that first time, and look how far it went. This time, put a bit of muscle into the skip," Becky said.

I traced my fingers over the smooth rock and took a deep breath. Then, I reeled back like a pitcher for the New York Bankees and unleashed my arm's potential. TCH. TCH. TCH. TCH. TCH. TCH. TCH. TCH. Tiny pieces of the rock broke off with each dip into the water, and it flew even further than my first toss. The rock left a larger impact on the water and even crashed through a wave as it darted forward.

That time I counted about 20 skips before it sank beneath the water.

With a huge grin on my face, I kept at this for the next half hour. I must have emptied the beach of rocks as my arm reloaded over and over, fresh stones in the chamber ready to fire. Eventually, I stopped tossing smooth rocks, hurling anything I could find into the water. TCH. TCH. TCH. That noise was music to my ears, and I kept the song on repeat.

"How do you feel?" Becky spoke for the first time in a while.

"Like I can do anything," I said, sweat rolling down my forehead. When at last my arm felt like I'd been jump-roping for 48 hours, I sank to my knees in the sand, jeans covered for the third time tonight.

I cradled my right arm and beamed. That was power. Power to feel in control of my fate. Power to stop being a victim. Power to put anyone who came after me in their place. Leaping to my feet and throwing my good fist into the air I let out an excited yell.

"Did you see how far that last one went? I almost made it to the boats!" I asked, spinning to face my aunt.

She crossed her arms and smiled big. It was like. . . for the first time, Becky had someone to pass something on to and the ability to share even a little piece of her vampirism. I understood a bit of the nature she walked around carrying every day. And the look we shared acknowledged that.

"Did you see?" I asked again.

The vampire took a few steps toward me and ruffled my hair.

"Not bad, Val. You got a feel for your new abilities tonight and explored them with excellent control. As long as you keep at it with this level of precision and awareness, then I have confidence you'll know when and where to really let the monster loose," she said.

As her crimson eyes locked with mine, I felt something new. Something that went beyond pride or accomplishment. Gratitude was mixed in there, too. Because here was an adult giving me positive attention, actually caring about what I did with my life. And I'd never had that before. Trying not to tear up, I buried my face in Becky's jacket and threw my arms around her.

She seemed taken aback by this but slowly returned the hug.

"Thanks, Aunt Becky," I said. But it was muffled by her coat. She still seemed to hear it perfectly and said, "No prob, Val."

We stood there like there for a few minutes until I pulled away and said, "Oh! You have to do one now."

"What?" Becky scoffed.

"Yeah! You throw one. Show me how much more powerful a full vampire's toss is compared to mine," I said, scanning the beach for another stone. As my eyes darted over the water, I briefly caught a glance of something bobbing in the waves watching us. But when I refocused my eyes, they were gone.

Weird, I thought. *Maybe it was the ghost of a fish I killed with one of those throws.*

Finally, I found what had to be the last rock on East End Beach.

Dusting the stone off, I placed it in Becky's hand, as she'd done for me so many times tonight. She looked surprised.

"Well. . . go on!" I said, clenching my fists in anticipation. This was going to be good.

Surprise gave way to a devilish grin, one that revealed Becky's fangs. Without reeling back as I had, she whipped her arm in a blur, as one might absentmindedly swat at a fly.

Her rock didn't skip over the water. Its raw force and momentum parted the waves for several inches on each side. Becky's stone carved a path through the ocean, leaving a perfect tunnel behind it for a few seconds.

My jaw dropped to the sand as my eyes strained to keep track of the damn thing. A large blue fish with yellow fins, perhaps the unluckiest creature to ever exist, leaped out of the water at just the wrong time. And Becky's stone cut it clean in half, leaving behind a cloud of pink mist and guts falling back into the water.

Oh shit, I thought, eyeing the carnage. But the

rock wasn't done there. It raced ahead and crashed straight into the hull of the biggest boat anchored offshore with a resounding BOOM.

Out the other side it continued until, at last, the rock hit the water, skipped 23 times, and then sank into a surprised ocean.

I flinched at the sudden noise, and Becky's eyes widened as the boat began to sink. The noise was loud enough to have echoed through the harbor. As we stood there paralyzed in shock, I heard police sirens in the distance, racing up Munjoy Hill.

"Well, my young niece. How would you like to test out a second ability tonight?" Becky asked, looking up and down the beach to make sure we were still alone.

But at the rate those officers darted down Congress Street toward the Eastern Prom, we wouldn't be for long.

"What ability did you have in mind, Aunt Becky?" I asked, a hint of tension in my voice. The blue flashing lights were now visible at the top of the hill.

Becky suddenly hissed, "Vampire speed. Go go go!"

CHAPTER 9

Becky didn't fumble with the keys even a little bit as we raced into the living room. A ticking wooden clock with several birds of Maine for the hours showed me it was around 4 a.m. My brown hair was a mess as my aunt failed to warn me vamp speed fucks it up. Think riding in a convertible with the top down but multiplied by 20.

I was pulling it back into a ponytail when Becky and I started laughing uncontrollably. And I mean, backs against each other, slowly sliding to the floor, silly laughing.

"Did you see how fast we were going?" I asked when I got wind back in my lungs. Becky gave me a high-five and said, "That poor early shift guy getting into his old truck, looking around for the source of noise, but we were already down the block. Oh, man. He's gonna be wicked spooked for a week, bub."

We laughed some more until a squeaking floorboard caught our attention. Standing before us in a silk cap and a blue nightgown was a scowling Jazmine.

"Uh oh. . .busted," Becky muttered.

Her eyes were fully awake, not one ounce of sleep remained in that fierce gaze of hers. I watched her sign to Becky. When she signed with me, Aunt Jazmine's movements typically had a bit more fluidity to them. Tonight, they were snappy and irritated. I had no clue what she was saying because the ink witch was signing so quickly.

Becky signed back with a cringing smile that pleaded for mercy. And for my ease of understanding, she spoke as she signed.

"Yeah. . .the cops racing through Munjoy Hill were called because of us. I was teaching Val about the limits of her vampiric strength by tossing stones into the ocean," she said. "And she got a little carried away, accidentally sinking a boat."

I gawked, heat rushing through my cheeks as I pointed an accusing finger at the aunt who'd just thrown me under the bus. Or maybe a train at this rate.

While I gasped in outrage, Becky's desperate smile shrank. She withered under Jazmine's glare.

The aunt who had yet to betray me signed some more, and the vampire nervously chuckled.

"I mean — it wasn't a big boat. Not like a yacht.

And, yes, I may have actually been the one who sank it. But let's look at the big picture here. Our niece learned a valuable lesson from this. She knows the limits of her strength AND speed thanks to our fleeing the police."

Jazmine's stare intensified.

Aunt Becky flinched under that raw power the witch seemed to be radiating. I suddenly knew all the vampiric strength in the world wasn't going to save her. And thanks to her betrayal, I wasn't going to bail her ass out.

Before I could chime in, my body rattled. The room spun. My shoulders seized, and I felt my insides collapsing in on themselves. A black hole had just opened in my stomach, and ravenous cravings washed over me.

I began to sweat and clutched my arms desperately in an attempt to keep from shaking. A small plea for help escaped my lips before Becky noticed.

"Whoops," she said while signing to Jazmine. "Looks like our girl is going through her first True Hunger. It hit faster than I expected. Fortunately, I prepared for this."

"H — how?" I managed to choke out, feeling weak beyond all belief. I had a sneaking suspicion a newborn baby could enter the wrestling ring opposite of me and take me out in a single round of combat.

All of that power I felt chucking rocks into the

ocean? All of that speed that carried me behind Aunt Becky the entire way home from the beach? Gone. Replaced with an all-consuming hunger that left my insides collapsing and my mouth watering uncontrollably.

"I put a few steaks in the oven before we left. I'm glad I thought ahead on this one. Though, I guess I shouldn't be too surprised you're like this after all that throwing and running."

With a burst of speed, I felt Becky carry me into the kitchen and sit me at the table. Another blur of motion set a big red plate before me and four sirloin steaks, steaming rising.

All I heard was the oven door closing before this meat appeared before me.

"I crave blood during True Hunger. And as I warned you, your body will crave meat. Lots of it, depending on how much power you use. You won't attack people like I would in a hunger frenzy, but you'll be extremely weak and helpless until that hunger is sated," Becky said.

Jazmine reached into a drawer and started to bring me a napkin and silverware. But Becky gently grabbed her arm and shook her head.

"Kind. But unnecessary. What we're about to witness will be bereft of table manners, sweetie."

My stomach barely got half a growl out before I grabbed the first steak and tore into it with a bite that would put a lion's mandibles to shame.

Good, was all I could think, chewing as fast as I could.

Then came another massive bite and another. Juices ran down my chin and over my cheeks, but I barely registered them. All I could think was feeding that black hole tearing through my stomach, demanding payment for the powers I'd used tonight.

The first steak vanished with a speed that people who compete in hot dog-eating contests couldn't match on their best day. I scarfed down the second steak even more quickly.

More, I thought. *I need more.*

And, fortunately for my tummy, Aunt Becky had ensured I'd get more beef. When I finished chewing the last bite of steak number four and stared down at an empty plate, I felt my mental faculties creep back into my noggin. As if my instincts had driven all thought away until the hunger was sated.

"Damn," I croaked, belching in a way only a swamp ogre could appreciate. "That was intense."

"Now you can give her the napkin," Becky said as Jazmine tossed one to me. I was mortified to find steak juice covering the lower half of my face, and I felt my cheeks flush with heat.

Looking up at Aunt Becky, I gave her a grateful nod. Her quick thinking had saved me.

"Is that — what you feel when you haven't had blood in a couple of days?" I asked as if the question might be taboo.

Becky sort of waggled her head from side to side as if to say, "More or less."

Then her crimson eyes found my own and stared deep with a warning.

"That was just a taste of my hunger. As you've just had a taste of my power. And that's why I won't even think about turning you until you're 25. There are just so many consequences to consider, my young niece. But the next time you use your abilities in excess, you'd best have some protein ready to go. Maybe pack some emergency burritos in your lunch just in case, not that I expect you to use your powers at school."

With the emergency past, Jazmine turned back to Becky and signed something that left the vampire gasping in shock.

"Wha — I am not irresponsible and a questionable influence on our niece."

Jazmine raised an eyebrow, signing more.

"And you are NOT the good aunt. We both are," Becky said, sounding jokingly offended as she signed back at her wife.

Jazmine crossed her arms as she listened to the vampire's mock self-righteous indignation. Then she pointed toward the bedroom with a fierce gesture.

Becky's eyes grew wide and she scoffed.

"I am a grown-ass woman. You cannot send me to bed early without supper."

In response, the ink witch dipped her head deep into the fridge and tossed her wife a blood bag.

Catching it with one hand and standing firmly, Becky tried again, saying, "I am a grown-ass woman. You cannot send me to bed early."

With a greater speed than I'd seen last time the ink witch worked her magic, I watched the lights flicker a few times before noticing Aunt Jazmine's arm was bare once more. And her eyes glowed gold with ancient magic.

Uh oh, I thought, covering my mouth with both hands.

Becky flinched as a low growl filled the kitchen and dining room. I watched as a 300-pound Bengal tiger walked up behind the vampire. With a lazy movement, she swatted Becky's hip and pushed her into the wall.

My irresponsible aunt glanced over at the beast and then back at her wife, doing a double-take. Jazmine wore a mocking grin with a raised eyebrow. It was an expression of victory.

"Fine! I'll go to bed early, but just for this, I'm not gonna — " she was interrupted by Cymera lightly swatting her hip again with a massive murder mitten. Pressed against the wall, Becky managed to choke out, "Yes dear."

Then she shuffled off to her room, mumbling something I couldn't translate even with my new vampiric hearing.

Jazmine and Cymera shared a knowing gaze of amusement.

The ink witch walked over to me and mouthed, "Are you okay?"

I just nodded as she kissed the top of my head goodnight. She seemed surprised to find sand on my scalp and walked away shaking her head.

"Also your wife's fault," I called down the hallway after her. Jazmine waved me off without turning around.

Showering quickly and crawling into bed, I spotted Cymera already curled up on my comforter, back against the wall, tail swishing back and forth. My expression soured.

"Is this going to be a regular occurrence with you?" I asked.

The tiger's expression said, "It will if I want it to be."

Despite the massive tiger curled around me as I put my head down, I managed to easily find slumber. I dreamed of tuna fish. They screamed and jumped through the water as fast as they could, seeming to flee. When I looked toward the shore, I saw my Aunt Becky, eyes glowing crimson, fangs extended, and throwing stones after the fish. One by one, she slaughtered them, and I could only watch horrified.

I awoke to the feeling of Jazmine lightly shaking my shoulder. Cymera was back on her arm.

My eyes fluttered, and I groggily realized I'd only been asleep for a few hours.

It was a couple of minutes before I could focus well enough to read the sticky note Aunt Jazmine left on my bed.

"First day of school. Get ready," she'd written.

My heart skipped a beat, and I groaned, face sinking back down into the pillow. Was I ready for this?

CHAPTER 10

The first couple of hours flew by at nearly vamp speed. I protested attending school with only a few hours of sleep. Jazmine tossed me an energy drink and wrote on a sticky note, "Vampire strength, remember?" And — fair. I didn't feel like I usually did when I only had a couple of hours of sleep.

But my brain still dragged a little, at least until I'd drained the can of sugar and caffeine that served as my pre-breakfast warmup. Two bagels covered in cream cheese and a bowl of blueberries later, and I was feeling a bit more awake.

Of course, everything changed the moment I stepped out into the sunlight. All that inner morning peace Aunt Jazmine had tried to inspire with a balanced breakfast blew out to sea. And most of what remained was bitchiness and general hatred for that yellow dot in the sky making my life miserable.

My skin didn't smoke or blister, but it sure felt like a cruel god had focused a magnifying glass at just the right angle to make me an ant standing on a hill, cursing existence for all of its righteous light.

With a fierce throb, my head felt like I was underwater the entire ride to school. Jazmine offered to escort me to the central office, but I waved her off. She signed, "Have a good day."

I rolled up to the front doors wearing black leggings, used Docs, a t-shirt with the name of a local lobster company on it, and a denim jacket. My hair was tied back into a sloppy bun held together with a pencil that was, at this point, much sturdier than me.

Aunt Becky wasn't lying, I thought. *Can someone put the fucking sun out?*

Hoping some sky giant would lick her fingers and then put the sun out like an old candle powered me through until I was indoors. I even made the little TTTSSSTT sound with my tongue for extra satisfaction.

My wish didn't come true, but the daydream sparked a smirk. I wore that grin right into the central office, shaking hands with the principal for some reason, and taking my schedule as I was walked to my locker, which I discovered was #93. My new lucky number? Guess I'd find out.

The boy escorting me had brown skin and wore tight jeans with a sweater that had the school's mascot front and center. A bulldog stared at me holding a baseball bat in its jaws.

"So. . . Arkansas. You've come a long way, Vedalia," he said as I got my textbook out for AP European History and a few other classes. "I'm Ramón."

He directed me down a hall, and I took a deep breath. All the cockiness I'd desperately clung to in order to avoid feeling nervous on my first day of school dissolved like cotton candy in water. And I was just a mystified raccoon staring at the pond, wondering where it all went.

"Yeah. . . long story. I won't bore you with the family drama details," I said, smiling. "Thanks for showing me around, by the way. I appreciate it."

We passed a couple of large restrooms and a smaller unisex bathroom with a lock that said: "occupied." My boots squeaked on the gray tile floors of the hallway.

As we walked by the lunchroom, I smelled preparations for the day, cheap pepperoni, sausage, and cheese pizza meant to feed 1,000 students at staggered meals. I had Lunch B, which meant I'd eat 30 minutes after those with Lunch A. As I understood it, we'd be hanging out in the gym for freestyle exercise until it was time to swap.

When I asked about it, Ramón shrugged and said,

"It's not as big a deal as it sounds. You can play basketball or walk laps around the gym. Most kids choose to sit in the bleachers and talk with their friends until the bell rings and the coaches tell us to go grab lunch."

After a little more digging, I learned Ramón had Lunch A. Fuck. So much for having a friendly face to sit with and avoid a "Mean Girls" situation on my first day.

"I like your boots," Ramón said, pointing to the scuffed leather with familiar yellow threads around the outside.

"Thanks. I like your bracelet," I said, pointing to the little silver chain he wore with several charms on it. I spotted a baseball, a trumpet, a dragonfly, and a tiny rainbow.

My guide grinned.

"When you're settled, you should think about joining GSA. I'm the president, and my boyfriend is our treasurer. We meet every Friday at lunch, and you get to eat in our super cool club room instead of the cafeteria."

"That obvious, huh?" I giggled.

"Sweetie, you wore a denim jacket and Docs on your first day of school here. I can only imagine what that says about how repressed you were back in Arkansas. But you might as well have parked your beat-up old Subaru in the senior lot and polished your 'my other ride is my girlfriend' bumper sticker.'"

I now knew what it felt like to have the color drain from my face as the sound of a toilet flushing played in my brain.

Eureka Springs was a pretty gay little town by Arkansas standards. But I'd never gotten to be out there as a gay girl. I didn't get to come home to my parents and ask them if my girlfriend could come over for dinner.

Well — okay, I got to try that once. But then I woke up imprisoned by a cult. So, I wasn't exactly used to it here. Being an out queer in high school here sounded good in theory. But we'd left theories behind and crossed over into the territory of practical application the moment I walked through the front door.

"Yeah. . .well. You got me. Sign me up for the alliance, I guess," I said, trying to avoid walking too close to a large window that overlooked a busy Cumberland Ave. outside.

"Great! We're always looking for new members. You single?" he asked in a way that managed to avoid sound prying and gossipy.

"Tragically," I muttered, thinking of Mika, who might have been wondering why I'd suddenly vanished from school. Did Ebeneazar call the school and give them a cover story? I was suddenly faced with the realization that I knew shockingly little about my own disappearance and what that meant for the people who knew me back home.

Ramón's voice called my focus back to the present.

"We have a few spectacularly single girls in the club. I could introduce you if you want," Ramón said.

That sounded like fun, so why did Purple Hair Girl suddenly pop into my head? We'd had one conversation, and it was a disaster. There was no way we'd ever. . . I mean — she might not even go to school here.

Only one way to be sure, I thought.

My mouth fired off the question before I even had the chance to think about it.

"Do you know a girl named Agatha, by chance? She has purple hair, and I think she takes art classes at the school over on Congress Street?"

Ramón stopped walking, so I did too, my heart sinking at whatever had garnered this reaction from him.

"Agatha Dean? Yeah, I know her. Well — 'know' might be a strong word. I know her name and a couple of assorted facts about her. She's pretty closed off."

Yeah, she is pretty, my brain thought, dreamily, not hearing the last two words of the GSA president's sentence.

Shaking my head to try and focus, I cleared my throat.

"I just, um, bumped into her at the bodega. Her father said she goes here is all. I was curious," I said, trying to play it cool. Did I need to make eye contact with him to sell it, or did I just stare ahead nonchalantly? What would convince him I was chill and not at all desperate for any shred of information I might glean from him?

Ramón nodded and mercifully decided to avoid giving me shit about it.

"You won't see her in the mornings. She takes a university art course for college credit. And then she comes back here to finish up after lunch. Sounds exhausting to me, but she's already lined up several scholarships for her work, so what do I know?"

Oh damn. She's a serious artist, I thought, trying to avoid thinking of ways to ask her to show me her work. Because that'd be creepy. And I'm definitely not a creep. I'm barely a vampire.

"Anyway, you might not have much luck with Agatha. She's kind of an ice queen. Not mean. . . just extraordinarily focused on her work and dedicated to being a loner. I've been trying to get her to join GSA for months. The most I can get out of her is a noncommittal shrug or grunt. But you know who is much more available and way prettier?"

I shook my head.

"There's a girl in your AP English Lit class named Miranda. She's drop-dead gorgeous, an amazing dancer, and our club's most eligible bi-bachelorette.

And if you're not into dancing, there's always Ài, our school's top violinist. She consistently places first or second chair each year in All-State. And I've had three different girls tell me Ài was the best first date they've ever had. Assuming you're cool with dating trans girls."

I shrugged. Why wouldn't I be?

"Girls are girls, dude," I said.

Ramón flashed me his most charming smile yet.

"You and I are going to get along just fine," he said, smoothing back his wavy black hair. "And I'll take any chance I can get to brag about my GSA members. They're all amazing."

Nodding and resuming walking after Ramón toward my first period, I felt a little more at ease. GSA sounded like a great place to make new friends. Ài and Miranda both seemed like a great start to finding my first official girlfriend.

So why couldn't I stop thinking about the alleged ice queen? The way she called me Coffee Girl and teased me without mercy. She wasn't even here half the time.

Theoretically, Ài was here all day. So we could hold hands walking to class or meet at each other's lockers, maybe even have lunch together.

But Agatha. . ., my mind kept thinking.

Once again, Ramón's voice pulled me out of my thoughts, my stupid distracting purple thoughts.

"Here you go. First class of the day, Mythology

and Folklore. The teacher's name is Mr. Duffy. And he's one of those guys who tries way too hard to be chill. He'll sit on his desk on Fridays and practice guitar. But he's pretty nice. You should ask him about why Bigfoot actually belongs in Maine instead of the Pacific Northwest. That'll get him going."

We said our goodbyes, and I walked toward my first period, suddenly feeling vulnerable and nervous again. My hands were sweaty, and my eyes darted in way too many directions.

"Hello darkness, my old friend. . ." I muttered, turning the doorknob.

Mythology and Folklore turned out okay after I flubbed an introduction where Mr. Duffy asked me for my favorite cryptid in front of the class. I almost choked on my spit trying to avoid the word "vampire." A few people snickered. But I took my seat and remained relatively invisible for the next 50 minutes.

The rest of the morning was a blur of saying my name to 20 strangers and sitting at a desk that just did not feel normal after 30 days of a hostage experience.

During freestyle exercise, I managed to follow a decent-sized crowd to the gym and not get lost while I waited 30 minutes for lunch. My stomach growled.

Quiet. I haven't even used any vamp powers today, I thought. *You don't get to sing me the song of your people unless I do.*

I found a lonely corner of the bleachers behind a group of girls who were talking about Katniss. Suddenly, it felt like I was once more a little girl.

"All that's old is new again," I muttered, checking my phone and fucking around for a few minutes on Reddit. I quickly discerned the Portland, Maine subreddit served two main functions: complaining about unhoused people camping and trying to figure out the source of mysterious noises at night.

Exhilarating, I thought.

A shout drew my attention to one of the basketball goals. The gym had two main goals and then a couple off to the side that were used for practice and folded up to the ceiling during games.

A girl was surrounded by about four or five larger guys. Her curly red hair shook back and forth as she told one of the guys "No." I didn't hear what he was asking for, but his body language suggested he wanted the ball.

Focussing on my hearing and straining my ears, I picked up his voice.

"Just give me the ball, tranny. That equipment is for the girls' team. You can go grab one of the boys' basketballs from the crate over there," he said, taking another step toward the girl.

My fists clenched upon him hearing him use that word.

The girl held her basketball tighter and scowled,

trying to cover up her shaking arms. Her knees were locked, and her shoulders were all bunched up.

"Fuck off, Dillon," she said with a strained voice. "You know I'm the girls' team manager. And even if I wasn't, do you realize how monumentally stupid it is to gender sports equipment?"

Dillon shrugged.

"I'm not gonna ask again. Hand over the ball, girl-boy," he said. "Unless, of course, you want me to take it away from you."

Dillon was wearing his team jersey and matching shorts. His trimmed black hair was spiked and looked like it consumed a metric liter of gel every single morning. He had the body of a ballplayer, thick legs, and toned arms.

His teammates stood around their prey like a wall of muscle cutting off any escape. Nobody moved to help her. In fact, most of the students weren't paying any attention. And she appeared too stressed and ashamed to call out for help.

I looked for a coach nearby, but unsurprisingly, they were sitting in a nearby office on their computers.

The girl's painted fingernails clutched her basketball tighter. And today was the day I learned the basketballs women played with were a little smaller.

Ice spread through my chest as I heard him almost whisper, "Go ahead. Call for help. See if

Coach Janet comes and bails you out again. You know she only lets you manage the team because the district makes her, right? They're scared of a lawsuit."

Dillon advanced on the girl, and she retreated closer to the wall.

"You know what, Dillon? You can have the ball if you can answer a quick question for me."

"What's that?" he asked.

I watched her jaw clench. She was about to throw gasoline on the fire. I'd seen that look in the mirror too many times growing up.

"Where did you learn that word?"

"What word? Tranny?"

"No. . . lawsuit. Kind of a big word for someone like you. Was it in the crossword on the back of your cereal box this morning? Kudos for sounding it out and saying it right."

A self-satisfied smirk crossed her lips to hide any fear that I was sure swallowed her alive on the inside.

One of the basketball players chuckled, but Dillon silenced him with a snappy head-turn and glare. When he turned back to his victim, the ballplayer's eyes were wild with malicious intent.

"My dad always taught me never to hit a girl. But since you're just pretending to be one, I don't think what I'm about to do will count," he said, popping the knuckles on his right fist.

"I'll try to remember that when I see your name in the paper. I'm guessing you'll go away for domestic abuse before you're 20," she said, defiant to the end.

Dillon sneered and drew back his arm as I suddenly stood.

Hate. Venom. Rancor. That's what I felt at this moment. Such intense animosity towards this boy did I carry that my fist clenched the handrail by the stairs hard enough to leave an imprint.

"When you wake up in the nurse's office, I want you to think about how angry you made me today and whether it was worth it to get your jaw wired shut," Dillon hissed.

Time slowed. I wanted to hurt him. I wanted to smash his face into the bleachers. There are 14 bones in the human face, and I wanted to shatter each one of them. He'd miss the whole damn season, assuming he ever played again. People like him didn't deserve to share oxygen with the rest of us.

Wait a minute. Did "us" include Vedalia? I meant people, right? He didn't deserve to share air with the rest of us people. But I didn't feel like a person at the moment. With a hiss and rush of power, I felt more like a monster. And I wanted to be one.

But most of all, I think I wanted Dillon to see a monster, and his teammates, too. They were complicit in this bullshit, even if they didn't raise a finger to hurt her.

Fine, I thought, snapping to attention. *I'll be a monster.*

Dillon's hand darted forward, aimed at the girl's jaw. And I appeared at her side without warning. Her green eyes were starting to move in my direction and register a new presence when I caught the bully's fist in my palm.

Two days ago, this would have left my hand bruised. But I was Vedalia Vamp now. I wasn't sure if this was what Becky had in mind when she made me her First.

Whatever, I thought. *Que Sera, Sera.*

Dillon's blue eyes widened in shock at my sudden appearance. Then he registered that I'd caught his punch with ease. It must have felt like striking a brick wall without warning.

My arm felt frigid, full of chilled strength. That ice spread through my veins to my chest and then my other arm as, in one fluid motion, I pulled Dillon toward me, threw my shoulder into his stomach, lifted him clear off the ground, and walked over toward a trash can.

I heard a few gasps in the gym as I spun the 210-pound ballplayer and planted him facedown in the garbage.

The trash can was big enough to swallow his torso, and it rattled around on its wheels as Dillon kicked and yelled obscenities. But it mysteriously held firm, not falling to either side.

Walking back over to the girl who stood there with her jaw agape, I said, "My name's Val. I'm new here."

The bell rang.

Perfect timing, I thought.

"Amelia," the other girl stammered, looking behind me at Dillon as he continued to kick awkwardly.

His teammates exchanged glances and then ran over to help free their buddy.

"How did you do that?" Amelia asked.

She stood there awkwardly in a lavender skirt and a cute matching top, sleeves falling just short of her wrists.

"Um, martial arts. Can you show me where the lunchroom is?"

I felt a familiar and creeping hunger starting to burble in the pit of my guts. And suddenly, I knew I could eat 74 slices of that cheap pepperoni pizza. Or sausage. Whatever they had that was covered in pork.

Amelia raised an eyebrow and then pointed toward an exit with her chin. It was in the opposite direction of Dillon, who remained imprisoned in his cell of garbage.

"Follow me," she said. And I did.

CHAPTER 11

A few hundred students sat around me and Amelia talking and eating their lunches as we stood in line. The cafeteria was set up to double as an auditorium and stage for when the Drama Club organized its play every spring.

One side of the cafeteria wall contained all the entrances and exits, along with a giant clock and speaker for announcements. Opposite of that was a lunch line. It stretched out a set of double doors that took you into an adjacent kitchen where the lunch staff plopped whatever you'd be eating for the day on your tray.

When all was said and done, I'd paid for three lunches so I could have six slices of sausage pizza. Amelia eyed me curiously while I grabbed a milk carton and a fruit cup from a nearby cooler.

"Wow. Normally the pizza here is bad enough

that eating one slice can send you running to the bathroom," she said, eyes scanning my greasy rectangles covered in burnt cheese and a spattering of pork. "But you willingly shelled out nine dollars for three helpings. What are you?"

"Hungry," I muttered, distracted, looking for a place I could plop down and devour this tray. My arms shook, and the tray threatened to spill.

As I felt weakness spread through my body, radiating from my abdomen, my vision started to narrow into a tunnel.

Where is a fucking open chair? I thought. *Just give me a seat!*

Amelia grabbed my tray just before I dropped it. I gasped, having not even realized it was about to leap from my arms.

"Are you okay? You're really pale," she said.

I mumbled something about being fine, but if anyone asked me exactly what words I'd spoken, I'm not sure I could accurately recall even one.

Fucking vamp powers really do come at a cost, I thought, closing my eyes and feeling my legs want to buckle.

Amelia pushed me in a direction from behind.

"C'mon, Vedalia. I know where we can go," she said.

I don't remember much about where she took me, only that when I opened my eyes again, I was standing in a large dressing room. Black and white tile floor, pendant lights above a long series of mirrors, and a counter covered in abandoned costumes and stage makeup filled my vision.

Behind me, along the wall, stood a massive clothing rack with black dresses in all different sizes.

"The choir wears those when they perform," Amelia said, plopping down a stool and clearing counter space for our trays.

I instinctively sat on the stool while she fetched another from over by a door that led to a tiny sink and toilet.

"Where are we right now?" I asked, my head swimming.

"The girls' dressing room backstage. It sits empty for nine months of the year. Nobody knows it stays unlocked besides me and the choir director. I come in here to eat when my dysphoria is bad, and I need time alone," Amelia said.

Looking at my pizza, I made a quick apology that sounded something like, "Sorry for what you're about to see." It might have been a slurry of those words for all I knew. What I understood for certain was how badly I needed to devour my food.

And "devour" might not have been a strong enough word to describe what I did to those soggy pieces of pie. The velocity, with which, they flew into my esophagus might have broken airspeed records. I almost waited for a resulting sonic boom. None came, but I was still convinced NASA had built rockets that moved slower than my pizza did on the way to my jaw.

As cognitive thought once more returned to my brain, I noticed my tray was nearly empty. My hands felt a little slimy. Amelia giggled and walked over to the restroom where I heard her cranking a paper towel dispenser. She handed me a few sheets that I guess could count as paper towels. But I also suspected that with enough friction, they could be used to light a match.

School budget certainly didn't go into soft paper, I thought, guessing the toilet paper here was probably single-ply as well. The monsters.

While I wiped my face with sandpaper, I let out a sigh of relief. My body was moving like normal again.

"That was an impressive display," Amelia said, nibbling on some crackers she'd grabbed from the salad bar.

"I'm sorry. When I use — I mean, my blood sugar. . . um. If I don't get enough, you know, vitamins, I — " I said before Amelia interrupted me.

"Do you want me to give you a minute to come up with a better lie?" she asked.

My eyes grew as I shook my head.

"I'm not lying," I said, trying and failing not to sound defensive.

"I guess technically you'd need to complete a sentence for it to qualify as a lie, huh? Well, you were on your way to one," she said, opening her milk cartoon and taking a drink.

To be fair, Aunt Becky had taught me about vampiric strength and speed. But she'd neglected to cover how I'd lie if I got caught using them. I suppose she'd just say to avoid the problem altogether by not getting caught. Or she could just mesmerize any witnesses to forget what they'd seen. Could I do that with Amelia?

No. I couldn't. Even if I might technically possess the ability, my stomach churned and threatened to return all the pizza I'd just swallowed at the thought of tampering with her memories. My shoulders seized with tension that the thought even occurred to me.

"Okay, well, while you think of a good fib, let's go over what I saw. You appeared right next to me in a blur of motion my eyes still haven't been able to make sense of. And then you lifted a 200-pound man over your head, carried him across the gym with ease, and dunked him into a trash can. Go ahead and tell me what you expect me to believe."

Shit. She was right. There wasn't a convincing story I could tell her to explain everything that came before my protein crash. What else was I going to say? I was too tired from the afternoon's excitement to consider the consequences, so I sighed and laid down my cards.

"My aunt is a vampire, and she gave me some of

her power. I'm still human, but for brief periods, I can move faster than your eye can track, and I have a well of strength that I haven't found the bottom of yet," I said, just as plainly as I might have explained the plot of "A Tale of Two Cities" or told someone what time it was.

While Amelia processed that with a look of pure contemplation, I ate my fruit cup, downed my milk, and stole another paper towel.

"Oh, and instead of drinking blood, I crave meat after using my powers. If I don't get it, I crash pretty hard," I said.

The girl nibbled on her pizza, nodding for a moment. Her stare left me wondering if she was looking at the wall behind me or five miles down the road. It was pretty broad. But without warning, she nodded, shrugged, and said, "Cool."

Silence reclaimed the dressing room.

I almost stammered.

"Cool?" I asked.

"Yeah, cool."

I just stared at Amelia while she took another bite or two of her pizza and put it down with a look of disgust, passing me her tray. After devouring her pepperoni slices, I washed my hands.

Sitting down once more, I started to form all manner of questions. None came out of my mouth. I'd just revealed I had vampiric powers, and somehow Amelia's response left me with more questions than her. How was this even possible?

"Why aren't you more surprised?" I asked.

Amelia finished her milk and cleared her throat.

"What do you want me to say? Everybody's got their own thing, you know? For example, I can't stop talking about Amelia Earheart once I start. I'm. . . kind of obsessed. And you have vampire powers. I'm trans. You have protein crashes when you toss jocks in the trash. No worries," she said.

I felt like the room made a quick 360. Had she met other monsters before? Is that why she wasn't surprised by my revelation? I guess I just expected her to. . . scream or run away. Maybe form a cross with her fingers and shout, "Begone!"

But, no, she was just sitting there, chewing through a salad that I thought even a starving rabbit would reject.

Maybe this is a good thing. She doesn't have a thousand questions. Because I don't have a thousand answers, I thought. *I'm not even sure what questions I could answer if she had them.*

"So, where you from?" she asked.

"Arkansas."

"What brought you here?"

"My. . . vampire aunt rescued me from a cult holding me hostage. Then she and her witch wife adopted me," I said.

Now it almost felt like a challenge to get a rise

out of Amelia. I needed her to gasp or her eyes to widen. A soap opera scream. Something.

"Wicked sick," she said, chewing on a large piece of carrot.

"You're very mellow," I remarked.

Amelia shrugged and started on the world's tiniest package of cookies. She wasn't going to give me an outrageous reaction. Suddenly, my brain finished processing her initial words to me.

"Did you say you had an obsession with Amelia Earheart?" I asked, cocking my head to the side as if that was somehow stranger than being adopted by a supernatural sapphic power couple.

My new friend's eyes suddenly widened as if I'd just asked about the secret to everlasting life or a winning lottery ticket. It was almost cartoonish.

"Did you know she bought her first airplane at 25? My Dad didn't have a plane of his own until he was almost twice that. And if that wasn't cool enough, she was flying by 1922. Think about it. While women were frowned at for wearing pants, she was cruising at 14,000 feet," Amelia said.

Her face took on a shine I hadn't seen yet, and it was almost inspiring to watch. The way her smile widened, and she gestured with her hands as she spoke. I didn't have any trouble believing my new friend was an Earheart fanatic, something I didn't know existed before now.

"And when she got sick? What do you think she did to pass the time?"

"Um. . .read books? Listened to the radio?" I asked, having no utter clue.

"She taught herself to play the banjo. When I'm sick, all I do is rewatch 'She-Ra.' But not my namesake. She learned to play a new instrument. . . by herself! Wicked cool."

I nodded. That was genuinely impressive.

Outside in the cafeteria, I heard a group of boys chanting something. I flinched when I realized the word was "Chug!"

"So, let me guess. You want to fly planes someday?" I asked, leaning back against the counter.

Amelia looked at me like I'd asked the silliest question in the world.

"I already do," she said, even calmer than I'd revealed my vampire abilities.

I raised an eyebrow as we exchanged glances.

"You already fly?" I asked.

"Yeah. I've had my pilot's license for almost a year now. Fly my Dad's plane about once a month. It's old, but she flies great," she said.

I did a double-take.

"You've been flying for a year already?"

"No, I've been flying since I was 14. You can get your student pilot's license then. Dad and I used to fly over to Vermont to visit my uncles all the time as a kid."

"Well, fuck, Amelia. That's actually cool. I don't think I've ever met someone with a pilot's license before," I said. "You must be pretty bummed they never found your hero."

Now Amelia's face grew solemn and stern. I felt like she was going to give me an even fiercer scolding than Aunt Jazmine gave to Becky.

"She didn't disappear, Vedalia. Amelia used the 'disappearance' to go into hiding and retire," my new friend said with all the conviction of a Death Row inmate.

"Didn't everyone agree she crashed into the ocean and died?" I asked.

"What's more unbelievable, that Amelia Earheart faked her disappearance to vanish and start a new life somewhere? Or that I was rescued from a bully today by a girl who's basically part vampire?"

I chuckled and stared at my empty tray.

"Fair point," I said.

Amelia stared up at the ceiling as her voice dropped to a near whisper.

"She lived in a world where society told her what she had to look like and be. A century ago, she flipped that world the bird and then flew off like one. I guess I hoped in taking her name I might be able to do the same thing."

I smiled.

"Hey, I heard you throw a bucket of sass at Dillon

before he wound up garbage-side. I think you're well on your way," I said.

Amelia turned to me and smiled. Her gaze still held some of that far-off wonderment as the bell rang.

"What's your next class?" she asked.

"AP Chemistry, I think?"

She flinched.

"Mrs. Addams. Good luck. She's a tough one. Fair, but tough," Amelia said.

We exchanged phone numbers, and Amelia took our trays, pointing me toward a hallway that went straight to Mrs. Addams' classroom.

"Thanks," I said and found myself soon facing a new classroom of strangers.

Mrs. Addams didn't make me introduce myself to the class, at least half of whom I'd already said my name to twice this morning.

We were a few minutes into class when the door opened and a familiar student walked in. My heart skipped a beat, and I felt my face getting hot.

"So glad you could join us, Ms. Dean," the teacher said, turning from her markerboard and raising an eyebrow.

"Sorry, traffic was rough," the girl said.

"We're five blocks away from the art college, Ms. Dean. Somehow I suspect traffic was the least of your issues. Have a seat."

My throat got tighter and tighter with every step

my terrible little crush took in my direction. She commandeered an empty desk beside me as Mrs. Addams sighed.

"Your seat is over there, Ms. Dean. Same place it's been for the last several weeks," the teacher said.

"Oh, but we have a new student. I figured I'd sit close and help her, maybe catch her up on where we are in discussing last night's homework on solvents," she said as I sank into my seat, hoping I could dive into a bucket of solvent and vanish.

Mrs. Addams rolled her eyes and turned back to the markerboard to finish drawing a few different chemical equations.

That's when I heard a familiar voice lean WAY too close and whisper, "Well hello again, Coffee Girl."

CHAPTER 12

*A*s Agatha spent the next few minutes giving me a rundown on chemical equations they'd been discussing, my brain felt like dynamite primed for detonation.

Pretty girl, I thought, shaking my head. *No. . . science.*

"And so you actually wind up with hydrogen and — " Agatha said, her hand brushing my arm as she pointed to a chart in my worn textbook. The book had seen better days. But it'd serve as good kindling if I went up in flames with Purple Hair Girl touching my arm.

Pretty girl who is good at science, I thought, using every ounce of willpower I had to focus on what she was saying and nodding at the appropriate times.

"Potassium goes on that side," she said, pointing

to my paper. Her hand brushed mine. "And aluminum goes over here."

Yup. This book. My desk. The room full of chemicals we sat by. It was all going to explode because Agatha kept doing that.

I flinched, and she smirked.

"Is something wrong, Coffee Girl?" she asked, mischievously. "Is the science a bit hard to follow?"

Her tone was dripping with meanness, but her eyes said, "You know you're having fun."

Was I? My chair groaned from how tight I'd clenched my legs around the edge. That only made Agatha smile more. And her grin continued to grow in cruelty.

I somehow made it through chemistry in one piece, and the rest of the day, Agatha showed up in every class. This did nothing to help my nerves or focus.

At last, my first day back at school was over, and I had so much pent up. . . we'll call it energy. I wanted to run a marathon at vamp speed. My chest felt exhausted from all the rattling my heart had been doing.

A little brush of my arm there, a quick, "Oop, you got something on your cheek. I'll get it for you," and even a light tug on my hair as Agatha remarked how pretty my natural color was all left me feeling like my world was spinning.

Walking to my locker gave me a little relief.

Agatha's locker turned out to be on the other side of the building. With a long sigh, I opened my locker door and got what textbooks I'd need for my homework tonight.

First day back to school, and I've already got homework in three classes, plus a fucking quiz tomorrow, I thought. *I wonder if Ebeneazor's cult basement was all that bad in comparison.*

At that thought, my lips tightened, until I snorted as a laugh escaped.

"We laugh because otherwise we'd cry," I muttered, closing my locker door.

Amelia popped over to see how my first day had wrapped up. How did I tell her my thighs had friction burns from how tight I'd squeezed them in class?

"Oh, you know, just average stuff. Homework. Teachers who regret their career choices. Feeling like the entire school is staring at me with a raised eyebrow. Typical new girl experience, right?"

Amelia patted me lightly on the back and said, "You're gonna do fine, Val. If you need anything, feel free to text me. I had originally planned to invite you over for dinner tonight, but my Dad texted me saying he's sick. So maybe later this week?"

A butterfly smile fluttered over my lips. Was this happening? I had a monstrous crush on a cute girl and a bestie inviting me to dinner on the same day? Shit. It was everything I dreamed of, not just in that basement when I didn't know what the future held, but living in the closet at a high school in small-town Arkansas.

Here, queer students didn't seem to draw even a single stare from anyone I'd assume to be cishet. Ramón walked by holding the hand of a real beefcake of a boy I had trouble believing was our age. He looked like a college football player. His alabaster hand held snug against Ramón's as the president and treasurer of the GSA navigated herds of students milling about in the halls.

As I spotted Ramón's boyfriend, I raised an eyebrow. And in my head, all I could hear was Schmidt's voice yelling, "A white man?! No!"

They waved as I giggled, and watched them disappear around the corner next to a poster for an upcoming talent show.

I turned back to Amelia and said, "That'd be cool. I'll have to invite you over to meet my aunts soon, too. They're pretty chill. I bet they'd love meeting my first official Maine friend."

Amelia's eyes widened just a little, like she was secretly waiting for me to spill the beans and reveal we were friends now. What else would we be after I tossed that jock in the trash for her? What companions had better meeting stories than that?

My new bestie turned her head slightly and waved at someone walking up behind me.

"Hey, Agatha! Have you met Vedalia yet?"

My heart kicked like a Muay Thai master, and I nearly choked on my spit, a classy move I copyrighted during my first week of third grade.

I felt her leaning on my shoulder before I saw her.

"Of course I have! And, FYI, Amelia, her friends get to call her 'Val,'" Agatha said as I tried not to realize for the 30th time in three hours that the girl standing irrationally close to me smelled like salted ice cream and sea breeze.

Amelia looked stunned at how chummy Agatha and I apparently were. And I must have looked stunned about the supposed ice queen using Amelia's proper name and treating her like any other girl here at school.

My new bestie looked like she wanted to ask something and thought better about it because she started to fiddle with the strap of her pink backpack.

I grabbed her sleeve and said, "Yes, Amelia, that includes you. You can call me Val."

Before I could say anything else, Agatha gushed and said, "But only I get to call her Coffee Girl."

Amelia snorted as I made a Herculean effort to put two inches of space between myself and Purple Hair Girl. As her gaze darted between me and Amelia, Agatha's eyes seemed to shine a little brighter in the light. But when I blinked, they were back to normal.

"How do you two know each other?" I asked, pointing to Amelia and then Agatha.

Amelia put her hands in her jacket pockets.

"Agatha and I have been friends for about a year now," she said.

Purple Hair Girl rolled her eyes, but not in a cruel way, more of an ironic, "I have a reputation to keep," way.

"I tutor Amelia in science," Agatha said, matter of fact to me. Then she turned to the airplane enthusiast and said, "Amelia, sweetheart, you know I don't have friends. Just — "

Amelia finished that sentence for her.

"Just people you want to drown in the harbor and people you don't want to drown in the harbor. I know."

My new bestie giggled.

"Agatha found me right after I came out as trans. My previous friends weren't exactly mean. But they were awkward about it all and sort of evaporated. Then along comes this girl who does her very best to be a loner here at school. And she just nails my pronouns and chosen name without any issues. On top of that, Agatha helped me get an A- in AP Bio."

I turned to my new seat buddy.

"So what I'm hearing is call you for science homework help tonight?" I asked, surprising even myself with the flirty tone.

Agatha, without even flinching, said, "You can

call me for help with lots of things. Science home-work, essays, boredom, whatever."

Amelia put her hands over her mouth, and I could have sworn I saw literal stars in her eyes. Her expression hearing us was the epitome of, "Now kiss."

But my hands were sweaty, and I felt like if I tried to take a step in any direction I'd trip, fall, and somehow crash through the Earth's crust, popping out in Australia. On the one hand, I could finally meet my favorite dog family. On the other hand, spiders big enough to eat birds and snakes. So, you know, fuck that.

"Well, I've gotta run to catch the bus and get home. I'll text you both later," Amelia said, excusing herself from the conversation.

When I closed my locker, Agatha hooked her arm in mine and pulled me toward the exit.

"C'mon, Val. We can walk home together since we live so close to each other."

Taken aback by the sudden feeling of being whisked down the hall, I cleared my throat, and asked, "You live in Munjoy too?"

"Yup. My family has a condo above the bodega. It's a bit old, but I have a big room. We also put a garden on the roof."

My heart continued to hammer like pistons in an engine (at least, that's what I assumed pistons did).

We walked outside and down a little alleyway

behind a parking garage. The sun was getting lower in the sky. I kept a careful eye on its rays as Agatha escorted me down the alley. We didn't hit a single patch of light, which earned me a nice sigh of relief. I still remembered my throbbing migraine from this morning on the way into school.

"What's got you so relieved, Coffee Girl?" Agatha asked. "Remember some more words after your literature class today? Going to try a new nickname for me?"

Heat rushed to my cheeks. I was about at my limit for teasing today.

"One time I called you Purple Hair Girl. One time! And it was just because you were one of the only people I really noticed when my Aunt Becky and I rode into the city for the first time. I saw you outside the art college with a giant sketchpad," I said.

She seemed to pause for a moment before continuing.

"So I was the first person you noticed in the whole city, huh?" she asked.

I nodded.

"Or maybe you're just invariably drawn to bright colors. What are your other interests? Shapes? ABCs?"

Pulling free of her arm, I frowned while her smile remained exactly as it was. And I'm not sure what drove it, but I suddenly felt a surge of pride and power. I'd tossed a 200-pound man into a trash can today. I could easily pick up Purple Hair Girl and drop her in a dumpster if I wanted to.

"You'd best be careful who you're teasing, you know?"

Agatha crossed her arms.

"Oh yeah? Why's that?"

Confidence came easy at that moment like a loan shark flocking to someone who'd been denied at every bank. My chest swelled on a cocktail mix of confidence in my vamp abilities and confusing feelings that'd been burning hot for the last three hours because of this gorgeous classmate. Whatever this mixture, I was drunk on it. And since revealing my powers had gone so well with Amelia, I figured. . . what could go wrong here?

"Because I've got vampire magic in me. Maybe you didn't hear, but earlier today, I lifted Dillon — " I paused when I realized that his full name was a mystery to me. "Dillon. . . Basketball Guy clear over my head and literally dunked him in the trash."

A flash of amusement traced across Agatha's face, and if I didn't know any better, I'd have guessed she was waiting for this moment. But that'd be crazy because she had no clue about my recent upgrade. . . right?

"Oh, wow. That almost makes you sound strong, Val. I'd better stop teasing you because I wouldn't want to risk the full power of a vampire being unleashed upon me," she said with no less mockery.

I scoffed.

"You want a demonstration? Maybe I can pick up a car or that pile of cinder blocks over there and juggle them," I said.

"Oh, yes, please. I'm afraid I'll need to see this legendary power you have before I can make an official decision to stop badgering you," she said, arms still crossed.

I rolled up my sleeves in a "you asked for it" gesture, scanning the alleyway for something to demonstrate my abilities. That's when my eyes fell upon a stack of wooden pallets. They had a bit of mud and oil stains on them but were otherwise structurally sound. They had to weigh at least as much as Dillon, if not more.

Walking over, I struggled to get a grip but finally managed to wrap my fingers around the bottom pallet. Agatha just stood there with an eyebrow raised.

Groaning, I powered through about six different protests in my muscles and lifted the stack, turning slowly to face the science tutor.

"W-well?" I stammered. "Do you believe me now?"

It wasn't the weight that was throwing me off, but the awkwardness of the stack and the angle of the top boards.

Agatha nodded twice but didn't seem all that impressed. Rather, it appeared she was prepared to mock me again at any moment. So I raised the pallet higher, above my head.

I wanted to pretend I didn't know what was driving my need to impress her. But deep down, I understood, even if I didn't want to admit it. I wanted the ice queen to like me. And some part of my cynical mind told me that Agatha's constant snide remarks were a sign that Val the Vamp wasn't one of her favorite people.

And I wanted to be one of her favorite people. Through all the mockery and teasing, I could sense there was a genuine care to her heart. If her typical reaction to people she didn't care for was to ignore them (or drown them in the harbor), then having her attention, even through teasing, had to mean something different, right? Maybe I at least had her interest? Or perhaps I was a desperate simp and seeing things that weren't really there.

That's probably the more likely option, I thought, struggling more with the pallet.

And that was the moment things chose to go wrong. Really wrong. A couple of rats selected this exact second in time to rush over my feet, and I yelped and hopped to the side.

Rats - 1 Vampire - 0

The sudden shift cost me any remaining stability in the pallets, and they came crashing down on Agatha with startling speed.

"Aggie!" I yelled, watching with horror as my

heart seized and sputtered viciously. The cacophony of wood meeting concrete and slamming into a nearby dumpster was deafening. I covered my ears and cried out for her again.

"Oh shit. Oh shit. Oh shit!" I hissed as the pallets finally settled. I'd lost sight of Agatha. Had she dove out of the way?

Tearing through the pallets and smashing lumber into pieces, I searched furiously, scarring up my hands in the process and drawing blood. But I didn't care. What if I'd crushed her? She'd need to get to the hospital immediately and — where was she?

By the time I tore through the pallets and got to where she'd been standing, Agatha was gone. All that remained was a puddle of water, which I didn't remember being there seconds ago.

And in the time it took me to glance around the alley two or three times, hoping against all odds Purple Hair Girl had escaped, ripples began to move across the puddle.

Without warning, a figure rose from the water — or rather — the water grew into a figure. And that figure was a girl. I watched it quickly take the shape of my crush who I'd previously believed to be in danger.

And then, there she was. Agatha. Standing in front of me without a single scratch. The puddle was gone, the last few drops absorbed into her sneakers.

"Wha — " was all I managed to say as Purple Hair Girl put her hands on her hips.

"I was going to be pissed you tried to kill me on our first walk home together. But then I heard you call me Aggie. You were so scared for me. It was adorable," she said.

I shook my head several times trying to make sense of all this.

She pointed to herself.

"Did you think you and your aunts were the only monsters in town?" she asked.

"I'm glad you're okay," I said, sighing in relief as my heart started to finally slow.

"Oh, yeah, I'm way better than okay. Sirens are notoriously difficult to kill, especially for baby vamps who've only had their powers for a day."

I raised an eyebrow.

"How did you know that?"

Agatha giggled and shook her head.

"You know what else was adorable? Besides you calling out my name in fear? Seeing you skip rocks into the ocean and getting so excited. It was like watching a child learn to ride a bike for the first time without training wheels," Agatha said.

That was her I saw in the water! I thought.

Looking around at the mess of pallets, the siren seemed to consider how fast I'd torn them to pieces to rescue her, not that she needed it.

"Though, if we're judging by today's results,

maybe you still need the training wheels for another day or two."

I couldn't help but chuckle in relief, taking another big breath and letting it out. But my heart jumped again when I heard someone unlocking a door. Glancing back, I saw a large metal door next to where the pallets had been stacked. Someone was furiously trying to open it, screaming about all the noise we'd made.

"Who the FACK do you think you are, making all that racket outside my restaurant?" A man yelled on the other side of the door. His accent was thicker than Aunt Becky's.

Agatha stepped close and threw her arms around me. Before my brain could short circuit, she said, "You wanna show me that vamp speed? Get us out of here?"

I nodded, carried her, and darted out of the alley just as the door opened and slammed against the wall. The last thing I heard was that man shouting.

"What a goddamn mess! My whole afternoon just went stove up to hell."

CHAPTER 13

Vamp speeding back to the bodega left me collapsed on the floor of Agatha's store. Well — her family's store. I guess she worked there part-time. When I started shaking, she ran over to the food prep area while I gazed up at bags of chips feeling weakness take me. I'd get better at this, right?

The cashier I'd seen before, Agatha's father, helped me up and half-carried me into the Employees Only section of the store. Before the swinging door closed, I saw Agatha busy in the tiny kitchen snatching five or six hot dogs from a commercial roller that slowly rotated them over a grill.

"I thought I recognized vamp speed dashing in through the front door," her father said, eyes reflecting light in the same way Agatha's did. The back section of the bodega was a little dim. It smelled of dried goods and dust.

A small restaurant booth with a table and tall wooden benches stood against the wall. It was old but clean, the wood chipped in several places. A bowl of condiments rested at the far end. Nearby, I spotted a mini fridge and a microwave. I guess this was the employee break area.

"We met a few days ago, but I didn't give you my name. It's Walther. I'm Aggie's Dad," he said, sitting down at the table across from me. I did my best to sit up, but my muscles didn't seem pleased with being worked after using my powers moments ago.

I cleared my throat and said, "Vedalia."

Agatha ran into the break area and practically threw down a tray of six hot dogs in top-split buns smothered with chili.

"Bless you, sweet siren," I muttered, finding the strength to suddenly sit up and inhale my food.

Walther tossed me a rag about 45 seconds later when all the chili dogs were devoured. I wiped my face and sighed in relief, feeling my strength return.

He told me to toss the rag in a bin off to the side. It was full of towels and work shirts. I did so and returned to the table.

"Thank you, Agatha," I said, rubbing the back of my neck.

She slid into the booth, scooting me over with

some surprisingly powerful hips. I didn't even have to move on my own. I was merely pushed to the side.

Heat returned to my cheeks, and if that kept happening around Agatha, I was worried J. Robert Oppenheimer would rise from the grave to study the intense chemically-powered blaze on my face.

"So, cat's out of the bag on my vamp abilities, huh?" I asked.

Walther leaned back and grinned. He had a great customer service smile that I sat on the receiving end of. He plucked a stray hair from his brown vest and shrugged, dropping it to the floor.

"I was a bit confused at first. But I've seen your Aunt Becky duck in here enough to recognize vamp speed. Subtle blurs in the air and the slight bending of light as you vanish and reappear are easy to spot for us. We've gotta have good eyes to survive in the ocean depths," he said.

It was now I realized Walther smelled of sea breeze and pine trees.

I slowly nodded.

"I'm confused about how you have those powers, though. I know your Aunt Becky pretty well, and there's no way she'd have turned you so young," Walther said, cocking his head to the left in a way that resembled a confused eel. "And the sun is still up, so I can't figure out how you're awake at this hour."

Flashing Walther a weak smile, I explained how

Aunt Becky had made me her First and gave me a taste of her powers.

He slowly nodded before standing up and stretching.

"Well, you can always feel free to rush in here if you're crashing or need a place to hide," he said.

"Or if you just wanna see me," Agatha said, sidling closer. "That's also an acceptable reason."

I tried not to flinch or blush any further, but this close, it was hard to hide anything from Agatha. Walther laughed, surprisingly loud for a man of his size, and said, "Well, I'd better get back to the register. You owe us $30 for the chili dogs."

Before I could turn to him in surprise, I saw Agatha glare at her father.

"Hey! The only one who gets to tease Coffee Girl is me, Dad."

He raised his hands in mock surrender and before opening the swinging door said, "I'll remember that next time I want to make a joke. Yeesh."

I motioned to the other side of the table and asked, "Are you going to move?"

Agatha closed her eyes and shook her head.

"Why? I'm quite comfortable here."

There's the ice queen again, I thought. *Wait. . . is it possible she's been flirting instead of teasing? No, that'd be ridiculous.*

I furrowed my brow, trying to shake the impossibility from my mind.

We chatted for a little while about homework and exchanged phone numbers. Eventually, I was released from the booth as Agatha said she needed to work the register for a couple of hours.

Before I left the bodega, Agatha smirked and said, "I'll text you soon, Val."

And she did. We texted a lot that night. Turns out, she was just as mean over texts as she was in person. I spent countless hours that night trying not to overthink what that might mean.

* * *

AFTER ABOUT A WEEK, I'd settled into my school routine well enough. I was daring to think my life might be normal again. Well. . . as normal as life could be as a girl with vampire magic.

I stood in the grass, watching my Aunt Jazmine and her band set up on stage at Thomas Point. It was actually a pretty neat venue next to the Fore River. Follow the river out a little way, and it emptied into the ocean.

A large plane flew overhead, landing at the Jetport across the water. It was painted blue, yellow, and red and had the words "Southeast Airlines" in large letters on the side.

Turning my attention back to the stage, I saw

Aunt Jazmine finish tuning her guitar. She was now talking with the keyboard player, a Black man she'd introduced earlier named DeAndre. They laughed about something and then took their places for the show.

A singer named Isabella introduced their group as Lobster Goddess. She stood illuminated by bright lights that danced across her brown skin and the colorful dress she wore. I could only imagine how cold Isabella must have felt, but as they got into their first song, she didn't look it.

Watching Aunt Jazmine play her guitar and bob her head on stage was an entirely different magic than I'd witnessed before. Lobster Goddess had a sound that mixed funk, blues, and pop. I was immediately drawn into their music when they opened with "The Net" and continued with a power ballad called "Loco-Cocoa-Motive."

Jazmine swayed and rocked as she played her guitar, eyes closed, and lost in the music. She drove their band forward with a mighty force that everyone else seemed to dance around and complement. Their bass player was the most average-looking white man with a beard. Everyone in the group just called him Guy. But he spent most of the next song smiling with Jazmine and trading places with her on stage. They even danced around each other at one point during a drum solo.

My aunt's locs were decorated with gold beads

that caught the light and swung back and forth as she swayed to the beat. It gave her this beautiful crown of light that would appear now and again, just to remind the audience of who was driving the car on stage.

The group worked their way through a fun little tune called "Radioactive Grizzly" before slowing things down with "Silk and Lace."

Jazmine got her chance to shine during an extended solo where she stood center stage after Isabella stepped aside. Up and down the guitar she took us, wielding mastery over every note and chord. Her fingers danced over strings at a speed I definitely needed vamp vision to keep up with.

The solo might have lasted a minute tops, but for that entire 60 seconds, nobody said a word. Out came the lighters and cell phones as Jazmine transported everyone on a journey entirely of her making, with magic that left Cymera on the arm that was plucking her guitar.

I enjoyed every minute of the concert and ran to hug Jazmine when it was over, and she hopped off the stage. A crowd of a couple hundred people shouted and cheered for Lobster Goddess.

"You were unbelievable," I said.

She flashed me a big smile and then shared a kiss with her vampire wife. Aunt Becky echoed my sentiments and had a whole series of compliments that she signed to Jazmine. They shared another smile before kissing again.

After the band broke down the stage and had everything packed up, we cleared out. Piling into Jazmine's car, Becky turned to look at her wife and signed something about going to get drinks.

Aunt Jazmine nodded, excited, and clearly still riding high on energy from her show.

"You good with that, Val? Wanna go grab dinner and drinks? We know a brewery that has great pizza."

"Hell yeah. What kind of drinks are we talking?" I asked, eyes wide with eagerness.

"Oh, you're gonna love this, bub," Aunt Becky started as my anticipation grew. "You can have so many different things. Club soda, root beer, or milkshakes."

I sighed.

"I was hoping for something a little stronger."

Becky winked with those crimson eyes of hers.

"When you're 18, I'll drive you up to Quebec, and you can drink to your liver's content."

That was all fine and good for next year Val. But present-day Val was annoyed with the sudden enforcement of rules by the irresponsible aunt.

"Come on, Aunt Becky. You'll trust me with vamp magic but not a beer?"

She shrugged, and I flashed Jazmine my most

sympathetic puppy dog eyes. She snorted and gave me a look that said, "Are you for real right now? You're asking me?"

I sat back in my seat and crossed my arms. Being a vamp was cool. Being a teenager was bullshit.

CHAPTER 14

Sand crunched under my shoes as I walked across the beach and looked over dark waters the sun had long since soared over. I was shivering and waiting for my supposed friend Agatha to appear.

She'd texted me directions to this secluded beach off Kendall Street in north Portland. I'd gotten nervous the beach might be private because it was part of a neighborhood, but I found a little staircase leading down to the water.

"Okay, secret siren, if you're not here in two minutes, I'm leaving," I muttered, rubbing my cheeks. November evenings in Maine weren't exactly known for warm temperatures.

Agatha hadn't responded to any texts I'd sent asking where she was or why I was here. She'd basically messaged me tonight and told me to show up.

No further instructions or details, no matter how many times I asked.

If this is a prank, I swear, I'm going to yell at her tomorrow at school, I thought, crossing my arms.

"Wow, I guess patience isn't one of your new vampire abilities," a mocking voice called from the water. And when I turned, Agatha stood, dripping wet, long purple hair clinging together in bands that swung back and forth in the night breeze.

She wore a gray T-shirt with the lead singer of Dismay at the Disco front and center and a pair of blue shorts that came halfway down to her knees. I caught myself staring at her thighs and quickly looked back at the houses behind us.

"Yeah, well, it's cold. And my Uber driver was listening to some religious radio station that had an angry, yelling pastor. So my mood's a bit sour," I snapped, perhaps with a bit more venom than I intended.

But Agatha didn't seem to take it personally. The siren dished it out, and she could take it. Nothing was personal, and everyone was a potential target for the mean beam. . . except for Amelia, whom Agatha weirdly seemed to dote on.

I'd been in Portland for a couple of weeks now, and our little trio had hung out damn near constantly. And the way Agatha could instantly shift gears from teasing me to genuinely complimenting Amelia on her nails or asking a question about flying with legitimate curiosity was almost a superpower in and of itself.

"I'll address your snide remark later, Coffee Girl. For now, come over here," she said.

Rolling my eyes, I took a few steps in her direction. She huffed.

"Closer," she said.

I scooted right up to where the water gently washed over the sand. Agatha had decided we should meet on a beach at night during high tide, so there wasn't exactly a lot of ground to traipse over before meeting the water.

"Does 'come over here' mean something different down South? Like, do Southerners genuinely think it means to get just a little closer to the person talking? Because, up here, it means to move your ass, Coffee Girl."

I motioned widely to the water all around us.

"You may be interested in catching pneumonia, Agatha, but I prefer to keep my feet dry. These boots aren't exactly waterproof," I said, wishing I had my Docs.

"Nothing you're wearing has to be waterproof for what I have planned," she said, growing more impatient.

I raised an eyebrow. Something about the phrase "what I have planned" didn't exactly inspire confidence I'd be staying dry. It sounded like I was going to be:

1. Drowned in the harbor
2. Splashed until I wished I was drowned in the harbor.

When I didn't budge, Agatha sighed.

"Do you trust me? Or do you just somehow have a massive crush on me while maintaining enough suspicion to make even people who lived through the Cold War think you're paranoid?"

I snorted at that.

"Cold War? Don't tell me you're actually reading that book from Mr. Jackson's class," I said with a lopsided grin.

Agatha crossed her arms.

"I know you'll find this difficult to believe, but some of us have enough focus to read books that don't center around the children of Greek gods going to summer camp."

Gasping, I jabbed a finger in her direction and sputtered, "Hey! They do way more than go to summer camp — " before I was interrupted by Purple Hair Girl holding up a hand.

"Stop. Whatever sentence you're about to finish is only going to embarrass you further. So let's just agree that I'm smarter than you in chemistry and history and move on."

Part of my brain wanted to continue arguing, but she was right. Any argument I could make about Percy and his friends would probably only serve to embarrass me in hindsight. And my brain already had enough humiliating memories to remind me of each night when I was about to fall asleep. It didn't need my help.

"Wait — move on to what?" I asked. "You still haven't told me why I'm freezing my ass off on this beach."

"And you didn't deny that you had a crush on me earlier," Agatha giggled. "If you'll just come here, I'll explain everything."

Opening my mouth but quickly deciding better on whatever dumb thing I was going to retort, I watched the water slowly recede past Agatha's toes. That's when I rushed forward and stood next to her.

"Be quick, please. I don't want to get wet," I pleaded.

"So, we've now learned that not only have you fallen hopelessly head over gills for a siren, but you also trust her not to pull you into the water and drown you," she teased.

"Aggie, please! The water's coming back. Hurry up," I said, flinching as a tiny wave raced up the beach toward us.

Closing my eyes and preparing for miserable, frigid, and wet socks, I felt Agatha quickly take my hand. Her grasp was almost as cold as Becky's when she was on day two of not feeding. My brain was trying desperately not to melt at the fact she'd accused me of fawning over her three times, and I'd had no comeback.

Taking a deep breath or five, I eventually opened my eyes when I realized my socks were dry. Glancing down, I watched the water hit the packed sand and then divide around our feet, as if a tiny invisible levee had been erected around where we stood.

Slowing looking up and getting lost in Agatha's amber eyes that shined in the moonlight, I heard her whisper, "See? Your trust is rewarded."

The water continued to retreat from the sand and then advance up the beach as the tide allowed it. My feet stayed perfectly dry.

"O — okay, you got me there," I stuttered, not sure if I should be focussed more on the hand-holding or Agatha's amazing control over the flow of water.

She grinned and then slowly pulled me out into the sea. My breath grew shaky, but the water continued to part around us.

"Shouldn't we be fleeing Pharaoh for this kind of thing to be possible?" I asked, looking at the dark water being held at bay around us.

Aggie held my hand tight and stayed right by my side. I felt power flowing from her full body into the tide around us. Her magic dripped across my skin with all the gentleness of a spring shower, rain happy to no longer be snow.

Nothing about the siren's powers felt forced or rigid. She hadn't built a brick wall between us and the sea. Rather, her magic drifted between bubbles and water in a continual motion, swishing the water around, above, below, and behind, but never letting it touch us.

She directed a current to carry every ounce of water within a few feet of us to the left or right of our direction. And while that swallowed most of her focus, Purple Hair Girl still managed to watch my expressions closely, looking to see if I was getting stressed or appeared afraid and needed to return to shore.

But mostly, I felt wonder alive in my heart. To see such magic on display, holding the ocean at bay and keeping you in a perpetual bubble was blowing my mind.

We kept walking over sand and rocks without getting wet. Deeper and deeper we descended until the waves covered us completely. The bubble was finished. It jiggled and blobbed but never sprung a leak or seemed frail.

"This is. . . unbelievable," I said, staring at the darkness around us. Above, the moon grew dimmer and its image more fractured by the waves. "I had no clue you controlled the water this closely."

Agatha seemed to wear a genuinely proud smile. It was a warm grin I'd never seen her carry before.

The ice queen thawed just long enough to appreciate my being impressed with her abilities.

"It's not something I can do forever. And making the bubble any larger would risk its collapse. But it's worth it to blow your mind for a little while, Coffee Girl," she said.

I listened to her heartbeat, and the exertion of this much constant magic and control left it pulsing as though she was running a marathon. Down here, her eyes constantly shined silver instead of occasionally flashing the color in daylight on the surface. It only added to the allure of her gaze when we locked eyes, and I stared in wonder for way longer than I had any right to.

"Look ahead," she said, revealing a bit more exertion in her voice as she worked harder to breathe.

My gaze followed where she'd pointed, and I noticed tiny creatures hovering in the water, stationary so my eyes had no trouble tracking them.

When we approached, a kind of bioluminescence kicked on, and the creatures revealed themselves as seahorses. I'd never seen one outside of a trip to the aquarium in Tulsa.

The little swimmers flapped their tiny fins to remain in place as a golden glow radiated from their skin and brought light to the seafloor we walked across.

My head darted left and right, giggling at the cute

little guys. Their skin was a muddy brown, lighter on the belly and darker near the spine.

"Keep watching," Agatha said, pulling me forward again.

Looking ahead, I spotted two more, also on our left and right. These seahorses started to glow as we walked near them, just like the other pair. And this continued for our entire walk along the ocean floor. We moved slowly, and I felt motion in the depths, a current I was more sensitive to as I stood entirely enveloped in Aggie's magic. It was steady and deliberate, a primordial energy that'd existed for as long as the planet had oceans that gave it life.

"Aggie, this is so fucking magical," I said as another pair of seahorses glowed to light our path.

She gripped my hand tighter as we walked past a patch of seaweed and a car tire half buried in the seafloor.

"I figured based on your complex interests in pretty colors and things that light up, you'd be easily impressed by the seahorses," Agatha snickered.

I fought the urge to roll my eyes, lest she pop the bubble and let me swim back to shore.

Feeling my heart start to pound, I took a chance and managed not to stammer as I pathetically attempted to flirt.

"I think given my obvious crush on a siren that my interests are plenty complex," I said, casually throwing my head back. "How many other girls do you know that can take steady verbal abuse from an ice queen and remain hopelessly enamored with her?"

"What you've just described, Val, is a submissive girl. And if that was enough to hold my interest, then my dating pool would include half the girls in our school, even a portion of the ones who'd swear up and down they're straight."

I scoffed.

"Well enlighten me, then. If you could berate and date any number of girls in our high school, then why did you set up a path of glowing seahorses for us to walk through? And come to think of it, how are these seahorses glowing in the first place? I didn't think that was something they were capable of."

Silence overtook the bubble. And the lack of sound was chased away by Aggie sighing.

"I've lost a lot of close people to me through the years, Val. I used to have a pretty big family and a large group of friends, most of whom were sirens. But through the years, hunters have steadily killed them off, mistaking us for predators eager to drown people and feed on them. Before Dad married Simon, he was with my mom. We lived in Connecticut and had a happy life there. . . until hunters found us."

My hammering heart slowed until it sank, and I felt Agatha's grip on my hand grow tighter. Her voice became colder as we continued to walk, passing an old shopping cart turned on its side and rusted to hell.

"I don't like humans. I think most humans are selfish assholes that are eager to see monsters wherever they turn and burn the world in an attempt to be rid of them. My dads are determined to keep me in school so I can have some semblance of normalcy, but I'm indifferent to the vast majority of my classmates at best and hostile to them at worst."

We stopped, and Agatha looked over at one of the glowing seahorses.

"These are called northern seahorses," she said, sticking her free hand outside of the bubble and holding it flat, palm up. The seahorse swam over and wrapped its tail around her pinky, resting in her grasp. It hovered there in the current, tiny fins keeping it suspended above the finger.

"Normally, they don't glow. But if I give them a little magic, I can coax them to put on a light show and line a path for a romantic evening stroll beneath the waves," she said quietly. A softness invaded her tone for the first time, and I found myself charmed by it. It was like Agatha put on this front every day at school. And, yeah, that was part of her. But down here, where no one else could see us, I got to witness a secret version of Aggie. And that secret became my treasure.

She let the seahorse go and brought her hand

back into the bubble. It left the water seamlessly and without even a single drop of moisture. As the tiny creature returned to its line, something far larger swam above us.

Looking up, I spotted a basking shark that had to be at least 10 feet long. Its jaw was open wide and swallowing everything in its path. As quietly as it appeared, it swam off into the distance and out of sight.

"I set up a path of glowing seahorses to impress you, Val. You were cute enough when you stumbled into my family's bodega. But the night you became a monster, and I got to see you swimming in new power, shrouded in fresh darkness, you became irresistible to me. I'm drawn to you in ways that defy any attempt I make at continual solitude. And if you dare to speak of these feelings on land, I'll vehemently deny them. . . shortly before I drown you in the harbor."

Why is the threat of violence only making her more beautiful to me? I thought, feeling lighter than air at the bottom of the bay. *But shit. . . she does like me. Never in a million years would I have thought that possible.*

Now that I had her confession, I wasn't quite sure where to go. So, I slowly took her other hand and just continued looking into the siren's eyes, hoping the gesture delivered everything I found myself too weak to say right now. I had the feelings. I carried the emotions and attraction. But the strength to say these things was best summed up in Error 404, courage not found.

So I just had to stand there in the depths and hope she understood. She got me, right? Agatha had to understand. She was wicked smart.

Clearing my throat, I struggled to even get out the word "Aggie."

And where I feared more teasing, I found only softness greeting me. The ice queen was gone, and in her place stood an unusually merciful siren.

She let go of one hand, and her fingers gently wrapped around the back of my head. Shivers raced down my spine at this intimate touch. But I sighed and let Agatha push my head down into her embrace, where the siren held my cheek between her breasts.

"I understand," she said with a hint of a giggle.

We stood there like that, frozen in the depths, glowing seahorses now swimming around us in a slow vortex. And I felt peace.

"Dating a monster isn't like dating a human, Val," Agatha whispered.

I shrugged, still in her embrace.

"I have faith that you'll teach me what I need to know, Aggie," I whispered back.

* * *

WHEN WE CAME ASHORE at East End Beach, I found a small curiosity swimming in my mind and turned to the siren.

"Hey Aggie. . . if you hate humans so much, why are you nice to Amelia?"

Purple Hair Girl ran her thumb over the back of my hand, and I couldn't help but smile at the gesture. It was like she was buffering, searching for an answer.

"She's been through a lot, and her struggles are different than mine. But I guess if I had to pick a reason, it's because society already sees and treats trans people like monsters. I've seen the way some people look at her in the halls and walking down the sidewalk. I've heard how they talk to her. And I've seen that kind of disgust and hatred before, in the eyes of hunters who took so much from me."

We stopped walking as I listened to Agatha's explanation.

"So, I guess if humans are determined to see Amelia as a monster, regardless of the fact that she isn't one, then I'm determined to welcome her as a fellow monster. I'll proudly stand next to her and tell them all to fuck off."

My smile only grew. I'd made a good choice in girlfriends, it seemed. Or. . . maybe she'd chosen me. I still hadn't worked out our exact dynamic yet.

We made our way up the steep road back to

Munjoy Hill still holding hands. And I was walking on air.

Agatha said goodbye and walked off toward the bodega as I turned onto the street Aunt Becky and Aunt Jazmine called home.

I was a few blocks away when the streetlight above me flickered and then slowly dimmed into complete darkness. The wind picked up and scattered dead leaves from a nearby yard, blowing them across the road.

Gooseflesh raced down my arm as I felt my breath go cold. Not Maine cold. Not winter cold. But supernaturally cold. Every exhale brought a bigger cloud of fog.

Ice spread across the concrete from a singular point in the shadows, and I suddenly found myself feeling entirely alone in the embrace of something deeper than the ocean's darkness. This darkness came from a different world entirely and swallowed me whole.

Colors drained from the air around me as I found myself entwined in a swirl of grays and granite.

I was still standing on a sidewalk, but my vision had just gone Sin City.

As I tried not to hyperventilate, a man's voice called from the ground below. And I watched a figure ascend straight up from the concrete as though he'd been swimming in the Earth under my feet.

"Well, well. As I live and breathe. . . the blood of Ebeneazar stands before me," a sassy voice echoed into the monochrome night.

The man, wrapped entirely in a black and red cloak that smelled of sulfur and molten rock, stepped a little closer. Wavy white hair that looked sculpted by an artist was the first part of him I noticed. As I took in more of the sudden visitor, I noted his ears were fuzzy, brown, and white, resting on the side of his head. At the moment, they were flattened and curved down toward the ground, almost like the ears of a buck.

His eyes were gunmetal gray, and they carried an otherworldly sense of malevolence.

I said nothing, feeling my heart racing and contemplating using my vamp speed to dart home. But would he follow? Did I want to risk sicking. . . whatever the fuck this man was on my aunts?

As the man smiled, revealing perfectly polished teeth, I shivered all the more.

That's when his cloak parted, and I saw him hold up a hand. A frilly purple sleeve dangled beneath his wrist.

"Now, hold tight, darling. I mean you no harm. I just wish to talk."

"Wh — who are you?" I stammered.

"You can call me Arsyn. And I presume you to be Vedalia, granddaughter of Ebeneazar, yes?"

I slowly nodded. What the fuck had my grandfather dragged me into? Why was this fruitcake of a man who melted out of the ground after me?

"What do you want?" I asked, trying to look anywhere other than his eyes. But my efforts weren't paying off.

"At this moment, I want a great many things, darling. A stroll through the Old Port. A big, muscled lobsterman to shag. A bottomless glass of wine coupled with two or three plates of lobster macaroni," he said, pulling out a surprisingly down-to-earth wishlist.

"Well don't let me stop you," I said, slowly pointing southwest. "Old Port's that way. Have your fill."

I'd hoped Arsyn would do just that, but he shrugged and stood there instead.

"Oh, those are things I want tonight. And I can get them without your help. But my long-term goal, the thing I've dreamt of for the last century as I gradually crawled my way back up from the first ring of Hell, is your grandfather's soul. He owes me," Arsyn said with a look that carried a hundred years' worth of wrath.

Stepping back, I felt like the air in my lungs had turned to ice. Every breath brought a deeper chill into my body.

"Relax, I'm not after your soul. But I do need your help to get close to Ebeneazar. He's warded his home and his little cult country club over the years. I guess when you exorcise a new demon every decade you learn a thing or two about how to keep us from knocking at your door."

What the fuck is this guy talking about? I thought. My grandfather? The self-righteous "it's not your fault" prick who was going to sanctify the gay right out of me? He was cutting deals with demons?

That didn't add up.

And the look on my face must have said as much because Arsyn shook his head in pity.

"Oh, dear, you didn't know? That's Ebeneazar's game, you see. I was his first bargain. For 10 years, I gave him access to power and wealth he'd never been able to achieve on his own. And when that decade ended, to the day, I came to collect. Such was our bargain."

At this, Arsyn's cloak parted, and his hand held a scroll bound by snakeskin. He pulled it loose like a shoestring, and the paper clattered to the sidewalk, spreading more spiderwebs of ice as it unraveled toward me.

I gasped, and it stopped a few inches short of my toes.

Before my eyes, an unfamiliar language appeared, written in living blue flames that danced and crackled on the page without burning a single sentence.

"Ten years of wealth and power in exchange for his soul," Arsyn said as I stared at the writing. The letters flickered like a candle on a breezy night. "Standard stuff. That's why I didn't suspect anything. But when I came to collect, Ebeneazar had planned a trap. Using his church and holy relics he must have spent his fortune on, the bastard exorcised me from this plane. And I dropped, as all banished demons do, straight back into the fiery pit, passing all nine levels of Hell, and starting right back at the beginning. Don't pass Go. Don't collect $200."

Arsyn was the only man I'd met who managed to combine sass with wrath. His words smoldered with rage and attitude that no mortal could match.

My mind spun with all this information. Was he telling the truth? Or maybe the better question was. . . what reason would he have to lie? I wrapped my arms around my chest to ground myself and work through everything.

"You said it took you a century to crawl back out of Hell and return here to get revenge, but my grandfather isn't even 70," I said.

Arsyn shrugged as if this was the smallest detail in the entire story.

"Time moves slower in Hell. It's how they dial up the punishments of damned souls and demons unfortunate enough to remain there. A lot of us fight to come here, sample your world's pleasures, fall in love, and live life where the air doesn't roast your lungs with every breath. And to remain here and get those things, most of us strike bargains with humans and send their souls downstairs. What can I say? It's a centuries-old business model."

I raised an eyebrow.

"But your grandfather weaseled out and got the drop on me. He did the same to a handful of other demons through the years. I'm just the first to make it back hungry for revenge. We have a contract, after all," Arysn said with a chuckle, tapping the scroll with his fingers exactly six times. It rolled back up all nice and neat, leaving only lines of frost on the concrete.

When I didn't say anything (because what was there really to say?), the demon pulled the contract back into his cloak. As it briefly parted, I got a look at his lavender poet's shirt, complete with enough frills to oo-la-la across Paris and back.

"So, here's where you come in. Sooner or later, Ebeneazar is going to come sniffing. He's utilized all that power and wealth to amass quite a little network that his cult uses daily. And all the vampire powers in the world won't be able to hide you forever. But, if you help me drag his silver-singing soul to the fiery underworld, I'll return the favor," he said.

Now it felt like I was standing on rapidly-thinning ice instead of cement. I wobbled a little to the left and right. My head felt a bit dizzy at the enormity of Arsyn's proposal.

"I won't give you my soul," I choked out.

He waved me off.

"Darling, I have no interest in it. Just your grandfather's. I'll tell you what. As a token of goodwill, I'll buy you some time, fuck with his investigation, throw dirt over your trail, and let you keep living the sweet sweet life of a teenager. Mazel tov on the girlfriend, by the way. You were both very cute together rising out of the water. That girl is going to lead you to places that you could only dream of."

My mouth suddenly felt like it was full of sawdust. And I tried not to choke on the dryness of it all.

"So... what? I help you fuck over Ebeneazar, and then you owe me?"

Arsyn shook his head.

"I'm not a fan of blank checks. We're discouraged from striking bargains like that, you see. It can come back to bite you in the ass. Didn't Andrzej Sapkowski teach you about the dangers of using the Law of Surprise?"

Having no clue who that was, I just shook my head.

A brief look of disappointment flashed across the demon's face, but it quickly faded.

He started again, saying, "No, sweet thing, before

we strike a deal, I get the exact terms of your desire word-for-word. Do you want money? College debt can be a bitch, you know. A cure for your aunt's vampirism? Some people do regret the change. You name your price, and I'll grant it once I have your grandfather's soul tucked neatly away in my little portfolio."

With my head still spinning, I opened my mouth to speak and found no words. How did one even begin to ask a demon for something? I supposed Ebeneazar would know. But I wasn't him, not in the least.

"I don't know what I'd want," I said.

Arsyn sighed and nodded.

"Okay, then. Because you won't find a more glamorous and generous demon in this part of the world, I'll still do what I promised. I'll go buy you some more time and return later. So think hard, little vampire. Because when I come back, I'd like to finalize this bargain, yes?"

I managed a weak nod.

"Excellent. I'll let you get back to dreaming about your new monster girlfriend. Tootles, kitten. See you soon."

And with that, he was gone. Color snapped back to reality, and I felt the hellish cold replaced by autumn's normal chill.

Turning toward home, I began to ask myself just how far I was willing to go in order to get back at

Ebeneazar. He'd held me captive for a month in a basement and prepared to brainwash me. But did that give me enough hate to damn him for eternity? Was I monster enough to strike that bargain and go through with it?

I had a new girlfriend. I had a new life here in Maine. But the one thing I didn't have was an answer to my previous question.

Wind traipsed over the water as our sailboat bobbed up and down in Portland's harbor. I took another deep breath of sea air feeling positively giddy. My hands gripped the side of the boat as Amelia came up and stood next to me.

"I think this is the best way to blow off class yet, Val," she said with a sly grin. Although, there was nothing sly about our decision today. Everyone knew exactly why we'd made this choice, and it was to skip morning classes.

Putting a hand over my chest and gasping, I pretended to be offended.

"Why, Amelia H. Vendalquin, I'm insulted you would apply such devious motives to my educational choices this morning. It was a huge academic sacrifice on my part to get that parental permission slip signed and miss four hours of key studies so that I might further my nautical education."

My bestie raised an eyebrow. And then we both snorted and burst out laughing. We were quickly racing toward December, and I'd worked my ass off over the last couple of weeks getting caught up on transfer homework and boosting my grades. Heading into semester tests, I was looking at all A's. And unlike the parents that gave birth to me, Aunt Jazmine and Aunt Becky seemed to give a shit.

It was corny as hell, but I'd even caught Jazmine hanging a recent history test I'd aced on the fridge. When she was around, I scoffed and crossed my arms like an embarrassed teenager. But when she'd left the kitchen, I'd nearly burst into tears over a couple of adults vocalizing how proud they were of my grades.

"Wow, and I thought that cult trauma had fucked you up so badly you might need a redo of your senior year," Becky said, and we both chuckled at her remark. Again, it was a moment where you either laughed or cried. I'd done enough of the latter in Dr. Dubois' therapy sessions over the last month.

Aunt Jazmine did not find as much humor in her wife's joke, smacking her across the shoulder and scowling.

"Hey! She proved me wrong, didn't she?" Becky protested, rubbing her upper arm.

Rolling her eyes, Jazmine walked over to me and

raised a flattened hand with her thumb out to her lips. She straightened her other hand with the thumb extended as well. Then, she lowered the hand from her lips and slapped the back of it into her other palm. After this, she made two fists, one on top of the other, and hit her wrists together twice.

Thanks to my intro ASL class I'd been taking at school, I knew she'd just told me "Good job." That earned her a hug, which was partially to demonstrate I understood what she'd said but mostly to hide the hint of a tear in my left eye.

My goddamn moms and their mushy emotions, I thought.

Amelia tapping my shoulder brought me out of the memory and back to the sailboat.

"So, out of all the students who cut class to preview school clubs for the spring semester today, which group do you think most regrets their choice?"

I rubbed my chin. I'd have said us if the weather hadn't been surprisingly warm today (for Maine), cloudy and 62. The water was cold, but then again, it wasn't like we were swimming.

Or walking under the waves in a bubble and holding hands, I thought, images of my first date with Aggie popping into my head. That was two weeks ago and three dates ago. So far, I'd managed to avoid fucking it up, which boded well for my lesbian sandwich card. I think after the fourth date we got a free sandwich. Or, more likely in today's age of corporate stinginess, a coupon for a BOGO half-off sandwich.

"Um. . . maybe the Chess Club? Weren't they the only group that had to stay on campus while the rest of us left? Bowling Club, Movie Club, History Club, and even Woodshop Club all got to head out and do something cool. Even the Bible Club went to see some a capella faith singing group give a concert in South Portland.

One of the Bible Club officers actually tried to recruit Aggie and me as we walked to chemistry class holding hands.

"Don't you two want some help getting right with God?" He'd asked in his white button-down shirt and black trousers.

We just giggled and walked around him. Aggie's laugh was great because you'd never suspect the ice queen to be so dainty in her chortles. She kept that laugh under lock and key for most of the day, too. But when you're dating a goofball vamp, there's only so much defense you can prepare.

"Okay, everyone come over here, and I'll show you a few basic knots. These are things we'll go over several times before taking the boat out of the marina next semester," our captain said.

She wore a wool pea coat that her long orange hair cascaded over like a waterfall. Rachel Kemestris was the Sailing Club president and had been out in this boat every year since ninth grade. The captain's green eyes swept over the five of us who either seriously planned to sign up next semester or otherwise were just looking to ditch class for half the day.

I watched Rachel tie her hair up in a ponytail and then pull out a length of rope.

"Out here, rope is one of your best friends. It moves your sails, secures items on deck from knocking around in choppy waters, and keeps your boat attached to the dock and waiting for your return," Rachel said.

As the wind picked up, our boat's sail flapped a bit in the breeze. Everyone's knees buckled as the Peaks Island ferry went by and sent a few good-sized waves in our direction. I watched people walking around the ferry and taking pictures.

"Wow, you've got good sea legs, Vedalia," Rachel said.

Score one for vamp knees, I thought, smirking.

"Thanks. Back in Arkansas, we'd go out on my grandpa's boat throughout the summer. That was a lake, of course. I'm still not used to how big the ocean is," I said, looking around at the horizon until my eyes came to rest on Bug Light.

Clouds continued to keep a merciful blockade against the sun, so I was in a pretty good mood, even humming a little until Rachel got back to her demonstration on knots.

Her hands moved slowly so we could all keep track.

"This is the figure eight knot," she said. And, of course, that made perfect sense given that it looks like a sideways eight was tied into the rope. As she demonstrated tying and untying the knot a few different times, I noticed Rachel had a small scar between two of her knuckles.

I couldn't help but smile and think of the Flying Dutchman's knots, wondering if Rachel knew the monkey's fist or the monkey's chain. Maybe even the monkey.

She didn't demonstrate any of those, instead opting for the slightly more useful clove hitch and anchor bend.

Rachel passed around a laminated sheet of paper with a diagram of our 30-foot boat. Well, the school's 30-foot sailboat. It'd been donated seven years ago by a family with many more boats in marinas here in Portland and up in Bar Harbor.

I found myself wondering if the boat my aunt sank belonged to them.

Guess we'll never know, I thought, shrugging.

Our captain showed us a few obvious ship pieces like the rudder, the boom, the hull, and the difference between port and starboard. Of course, I'd forgotten that last part at least three times and had to keep asking.

Maybe the Sailing Club isn't for me, I thought, gazing over at the Casco Bay Bridge.

"You know, it actually replaced a structure called

the Million Dollar Bridge," Amelia said, pointing where the drawbridge had raised for another sailboat going underneath.

"Why did they call it the Million Dollar Bridge?" I asked.

Amelia gave me a flat look.

"Because. . . it cost a million dollars to build," she whispered.

Vamp knees, vamp speed, and vamp strength, but no vamp brain, I thought, lightly slapping my face.

My bestie giggled and lightly patted me on the shoulder.

"Amelia Earhart made an emergency landing on a bridge half that size once," she said, pointing at the structure again.

My eyes widened trying to picture how difficult that must have been.

"Really?"

"No," she said, snorting. "I just give you so many Amelia Earhart facts that I wanted to see if you'd automatically believe me making one up on the spot."

I sighed and leaned in close for a whisper.

"Would you like to see if I'm capable of throwing you from this boat all the way to Bug Light?"

Amelia's face paled for a moment, but then she grinned in what I could only describe as absolute confidence.

"You wouldn't," Amelia said.

"Are you sure?" I asked.

"The only thing I'm more sure of is my gender," she said, crossing her arms.

I giggled a little at that. Then I tried to figure out the source of Amelia's newfound surety that I wouldn't toss her overboard with vamp strength. Of course, I came up with nothing.

"You can't throw me off the boat because you know Agatha would drown you in the harbor," Amelia said.

Now I crossed my arms.

"You're so sure my girlfriend would take your side in this?" I asked, a crooked grin sneaking onto the side of my lips. I still got a giddy feeling at calling Aggie my girlfriend. You could sneak the title into so many sentences.

"My girlfriend and I had lunch today."

"Aunt Jazmine, do you mind if I stay over at my girlfriend's house tonight?"

"That's so funny. The other day my girlfriend said something like that."

And each one made me smile like an absolute doofus. I was sure it mortified the ice queen to no end. But I didn't care. Because she was still my partner through it all.

Amelia practically beamed as she said, "I'm Agatha's best friend. And she can talk all day long about how she'll drown people in the harbor. But at the end of the day, if I was in trouble, she'd go to war for me. No hesitation."

Warmth spread through my heart as I considered Amelia's words. And I knew she was right. I recalled what Agatha had told me on our first date.

"If humans are determined to see Amelia as a monster, regardless of the fact that she isn't one, then I'm determined to welcome her as a fellow monster. I'll proudly stand next to her and tell them all to fuck off," she'd told me.

I'd chosen good people. Or maybe they'd chosen me. After a month in Portland, that still wasn't clear to me.

Our chaperone was a bus driver who doubled as a sailing coach. His name was Mr. Kelly. Ex-Navy, retired, and just kind of taking it easy and filling his free time by working for the school. I'd only met him today, but he was plenty chill. He had a bit of a beer gut and kept his blond hair cut short. He wore an eyepatch, but nobody dared to make a pirate joke.

Mr. Kelly generally stayed quiet and let Rachel do all the talking and teaching. At this point, he was just there to make sure nothing disastrous happened and that the kids had someone to look out for them.

I'd almost forgotten he was on the boat when he suddenly called out.

"Hey Rachel, there's a diver over there. I think he needs help. Let's move the boat over," he said, voice still calm but carrying a tone that relayed years of authority.

Until now, the only thing he'd said to our group was to make sure we had our life jackets on. All of us did.

Our captain swung into action while the rest of us did our best to stay out of the way. I turned to spy a diver about 50 yards ahead, almost halfway between Portland and SoPo.

The diver was dressed in black gear and had his mask off, waving at us.

A couple of minutes later, he was onboard.

I'd moved up to the ship's bow to give Rachel and Mr. Kelly room as they dragged the diver aboard. He must have been in his 40s. Giant drops of water dripped down from his messy black curls. The diver was coughing and tossed his mask and fins aside to lie on his back. He had a little waterproof satchel clipped to his side that instantly caught my eye.

Mr. Kelly ushered the other students into the ship's cabin, seeming to forget about me. I just continued to watch, perched on the bow pulpit, pulling a reverse Titanic pose.

The diver sputtered and thanked Mr. Kelly for his help.

"Oh man, that was a close one. My tank got tangled in a net down there and came free. I think a strap broke or something," the man said with a baritone voice. His accent was Cajun which made him a little hard to understand, but the thing that wasn't adding up for me was his heart rate.

For a man who'd nearly drowned and just been pulled to safety, his heart was eerily calm. I watched the diver's brown eyes lock with my own, and there was a chilliness there that nearly stole my breath. He was human and made a show of his hands shaking as Mr. Kelly asked him a few questions.

I spotted a silver wedding band on his left finger as he took his gloves off, showing ivory skin.

"Thank goodness you saw me. I didn't have the lung capacity to yell for help, couldn't even tell where the shoreline was because everything was spinning," the diver said.

Mr. Kelly cocked his head to the side.

"Did you launch from a boat near here?" he asked, looking around.

Rachel had gone below deck to check on the other students, and while our chaperone was searching for the diver's boat, I suddenly felt my heart caught in my throat. In a split second, the diver's coughing, panicking act was gone. He lifted his leg and kicked Mr. Kelly in the chest, knocking him back. I watched our chaperone fall backward into the cabin.

Oh shit, I thought. *Who the hell is this guy?*

Before I could react, he reached into the bag at his side and pulled out a gray metal canister.

Yanking out a pin, he tossed it down into the cabin and sealed it before anyone could get out.

"Amelia!" I yelled, preparing to rush forward with every ounce of vamp speed I could muster. But this guy was quick and had his hand back in the bag before I could say Nosferatu.

Next thing I knew, he had a silver cross on a chain pulled free of the satchel. I'd only made it halfway to the stern when that damn thing lit up with a familiar glow. It was the same bright silver light I'd seen in Indiana.

Blistering heat raced up and down my arms and face, and I hissed, kneeling on the boat floor in so much pain. Smoke rose from my skin and billowed up toward the main sail. It felt like someone had taken a bucket of lava and tossed it all over me. I couldn't move.

At that point, Becky's words came back to me, "Sanctified silver will also be able to hurt you quite a bit."

Yeah, no shit, I thought, hissing more and blinking tears that quickly evaporated.

"Well, Vedalia. I don't think this could have gone any better than it did," the diver said.

"Who the fuck are you?" I yelled as more smoke raced over my arms.

"Name's Blake. And I'm someone who knows how to speak without using language. Mother Mary and Joseph. . . Ebeneazar has his work cut out between the cursing and your vampiric contamination. You know, he told me you'd all but stopped cursing down in that basement after four or five days. I wonder how long it'll take him to break you of the habit this time," he said.

Flashes of that damn basement came rushing back into my mind, and at once, the pieces of the puzzle flew together.

I guess Arsyn bought me as much time as he could, I thought. *Two weeks wasn't bad.*

Squinting, I managed to get one eye open and scowling at the man holding a sanctified silver cross. Where did you even get those, anyway? I'd walked past churches in Portland without my skin smelling like hashbrowns so burnt they'd set off a smoke detector.

"Stop me if I've got this wrong. Grandpa finds a dead cult member and notices I've escaped. And instead of letting go and moving on with his life, he doubles down on this toxic obsession, puts out a hit with some Red Card hunters, and here you are to drag me back to Harrison after faking a little diving emergency."

"You see, Vedalia? You're plenty smart, which is why your actions confuse me so. Unless you tell me that you've been mesmerized, I have no idea why you'd run off with a bloodsucker and pretend to be in a little family of abominations."

That touched a nerve, and I managed to rise to

my feet, snarling. You didn't refer to the women who'd given me my life back as abominations.

"Why can't he just let me live? I don't want him around me!"

Blake shrugged.

"I don't know or care. I only met your grandfather a few days ago."

"Cult," I corrected.

"Church," he reestablished. "I'm just happy to reconnect a lonely grandfather with his misguided granddaughter. I have no doubt he'll set you straight."

They all talked the same. Ebeneazar, Blake, and every other member of this goddamn cult. It was like I had no status to them unless I was doing what they wanted. The moment I stepped out of line, I ceased to be a thinking, reasoning human capable of making her own choices. That built more fury in my chest, but goddamn that cross burnt something fierce. Blake took another step forward, and the cross' abominable light drove me to my knees again.

All that heat from my blistering flesh was sinking into my muscles and bones, the worst kind of inflammation. Aches of every sort traveled up and down my veins and joints. It was a regular pain parade.

"If it helps you feel better, girl, your classmates are fine. They'll wake up in a few hours and wonder what the heck happened. By then, I imagine you'll be in my trunk and well past the New Hampshire state line.

My heart hammered at the thought. The trunk of a car sounded even worse than a church basement. Aunt Becky and Aunt Jazmine wouldn't have a clue what'd happened to me. I teared up again, feeling the water evaporate as soon as it ran a couple of inches down my cheek.

"It'll be okay," Blake said. "He knows how to fix you."

There it was again. I was just damaged goods apparently, a busted radio in a thrift store just waiting for the right man to disassemble me, solder some wires, and put me back together good as new, playing beautiful music.

Help, I thought, pleading in my mind to no one in particular. We were hundreds of feet from shore, and everyone else in this boat was out cold. All the vampiric power in the world was useless to me in the gaze of this fucking craft store relic.

Blake took another step forward. Holding the cross with one hand, he reached into his bag and pulled out a set of handcuffs with the other.

My lungs felt paralyzed like no words could ever leak out and reach someone to help me. All I knew was pain again. Short ragged breaths and sizzling flesh were all I heard.

And then there was a small splash. With my one

good eye squinting on Blake, I saw a figure shoot out of the water and land on the boat next to him.

"You're not taking my fucking girlfriend anywhere!" she yelled and drew back her head. Her collarbones expanded as her chest took in all the air it could. Silver veins lined her neck as Aggie placed her mouth right next to Blake's ear and shrieked.

My god, it hurt, even from this distance, and focused away from me. She poured every ounce of her magic into that siren song, and I could actually see shockwaves pulsing around Blake's face. He dropped the cross, and it went spilling over into the ocean, ending my torment.

Now Blake was on his knees and screaming, though I couldn't hear him. I just saw his eyes rolling back into his head as blood poured from his ears. Then it dripped from his eye sockets as well.

I watched wood on the ship's cabin splinter and cracks spread along the length of the craft. The main sail shredded from the intensity, and the boom groaned under the pressure of Aggie's soundwaves.

After half a minute or so, Blake fell forward on the boat, and I collapsed in the opposite direction. It took a minute or two for my ears to stop ringing. I imagined vamp healing was rebuilding the tiny hairs and tubes in my ears.

When I could focus on my surroundings again, my eyes darted up and met Aggie's gaze. All I could do was whimper out a tiny thanks as she held me tight. The boat continued to bob gently in the waves, and I couldn't stop shaking. Aggie pulled my sleeves down over the blistered flesh on my arms. It'd slowly begun healing in the absence of that fucking sanctified silver.

I think Aggie pulled out her phone and called Aunt Jazmine, but I wasn't sure. My eyes fluttered as my head slumped against her shoulders.

"You're okay, Val. I won't let them take you," the siren whispered.

Amelia's words filtered back into my mind. She'd said, "But at the end of the day, if I was in trouble, she'd go to war for me."

I'd seen that today. She'd sniffed out a hunter and murdered him to save me. Because that's what monsters did. Sometimes they killed people. Aunt Becky killed a man to get me out of Ebeneazar's cult. And now Aggie had killed a man to keep me from being dragged back to that same cult.

As my eyes stayed closed for longer and longer each time I shut them, I sighed and finally passed out in my girlfriend's arms, feeling safe enough to do so.

One thing was sure. I didn't think I wanted to join the Sailing Club now.

CHAPTER 16

The chair was stiff. I didn't much care for how it creaked and groaned when I leaned back in it, either. I couldn't remember how long I'd been sitting in this nondescript room when it suddenly occurred to me that I also couldn't remember entering the room.

White walls with blank posters, a table with no scuffs or markings, and a blue carpet that didn't feel real when I ran my toes over it.

What the fuck? I thought. *Where am I?*

Looking over, I spotted a door. It was as bland as the rest of this place, beige, pine, and utterly forgettable. But the man who walked through the door wasn't forgettable. I'd seen him before.

His poofy white hair and gray eyes revealed themselves as the demon took his hood down. The rest of his black and red cloak hung loose but covered his body well. He could have been chubby, ripped, or simply well-toned, and I had no clue.

The smell of molten rock and sulfur soon filled the room, which I noticed had no windows.

"Arsyn? What are you doing… wherever this is?"

He sighed and sat at the small round table across from me. His eyes looked more weary than the last time we'd spoken.

"Sorry to show up unannounced, darling. You're dreaming, and I needed to speak with you again," he said.

Memories of the previous day's excitement hopped to the forefront of my mind like an angry chirping bird demanding attention. I caught a glimpse of a damaged sailboat, a cute siren, Jazmine and later Becky showing up, a few members of the Coast Guard asking questions, and then a quiet ride back to the house.

"Busy day?" Arsyn asked, crossing his legs.

I nodded and held my head.

"Ebeneazar sent a hunter after me. I'd be in the trunk of a car on the way to Arkansas now if it weren't for the intervention of my girlfriend," I said, rubbing my temples.

Arsyn smiled.

"I ran into a couple hunters myself. Sorry I couldn't buy you any more time, kitten. Your grandfather has grown considerably more powerful and influential since last we met. I nearly lost my own head planting a false trail in Colorado for him to waste resources on. The hunters he's hired are considerably more intelligent and ruthless than when we made our bargain decades ago. Your entire world feels different... like someone sped it up."

There was another exhausted sigh from the demon as he popped his neck to the left and groaned.

"I appreciate the help you gave me, Arsyn. Before that asshat showed up yesterday, I'd actually been having the time of my life. Three dates with a girl who makes my toes tingle with every touch, a sleepover with my new bestie, and a mountain of homework reduced to an anthill. Things were going great."

Was I imagining things, or did this demon that literally crawled out of Hell two weeks ago seem pleased to hear my life had been gradually improving since our parting? His smile was so much warmer than when we initially met. And the way his head tilted as he listened to me rattle off each detail in my more recent good fortune seemed to hint he was interested at the very least.

"But life caught up," he whispered. "I'm glad you've been doing well, darling. I had a few good nights myself in Kansas City. Met this painter in town visiting from Paris. Delicious little treat of a man. Coffee turned into dinner turned into a night at his place. I hadn't had that much fun in a century," he said, staring off into space, likely daydreaming of his artist.

I snickered.

"Hey! Don't daydream in my… nightdream. You might break physics or something. Leonardo DiCaprio will have to come in and save us."

Arsyn grinned.

"Another tasty dish I wouldn't mind sampling," he muttered.

What the fuck was happening? Was I making small talk with an actual demon? The kind of underworld spawn that bargained for souls? Crowley was going to be pissed if I made a new bestie out of his twink salesman.

But… talking to him didn't feel threatening. It was supposed to, right? Shouldn't I be terrified out of my mind? It was harder to get more "monster" than being a demon. And here we were just talking about our lives without a care in the world. That didn't seem right.

Maybe because I was raised to expect monsters to look and behave a certain way, I thought. *And now that I'm face-to-face with a few of them… the math isn't adding up.*

Leaning back in his chair a little, Arsyn studied me and raised an eyebrow.

"You seem to have so many thoughts swimming around in that fishpond of a head, darling. Care to share one?"

"What do I get in return?" I asked, winking.

"Oh no, the little vampire has figured out my game. I really have lost my touch," the demon said, raising a hand to his head in a "woe is me" gesture.

I chuckled, then watched his smile remain while mine washed away. Someone pulled up the stopper on my bathtub of amusement, and now the joy was swirling down a drain almost big enough to worry Tommy and Chuckie.

"He's not going to stop coming after me, is he?" I asked.

Arsyn's eyes watched mine closely. And the reply he gave was flat as could be.

"No, kitten. He isn't. You remain a proverbial thorn in his side every minute you aren't a happy little brainwashed member of his cult. Ebeneazar wants nothing more than to break you, marry you off to one of the upcoming youth in his sect once you turn 18, and get you popping out grandbabies to continue his bloodline. The joys of being an only child. And his only grandchild," Arsyn said.

The demon wasn't teasing me but giving me a glimpse of my future as he'd seen in Ebeneazar's mind.

I leaned over on the table, head in my hands, feeling rage and nausea well up in my heart. My chest was a bottle of shaken soda that nobody would pull the cap off to relieve pressure.

"Is this the part where you remind me of your offer to deal with him once and for all?" I asked.

Arsyn shrugged.

"You've just proven it remains front and center in your mind. I don't need to remind you. If you want the deal, you'll make it on your own time. I'm not here to rush you," he said.

Groaning and scratching the back of my head, I'd reached peak pitiful. I was a teenager! I wasn't supposed to be dealing with cults and abductions. My biggest worry was supposed to be acne and accidental pregnancy. Though, being gay lowered the threat of that second one considerably.

I propped my chin on the table and looked up at the demon. He said nothing. His expression was patient.

"If I asked you to leave and never return, what would you do?"

"Wish you all the best and then return to my boy toy in KC," he said.

Leaning back in my chair again and letting my arms drop, I looked up at the ceiling. I wanted two things right now. A button that would automatically jettison my grandfather to the moon from anywhere on the planet and a double date with Arsyn and Aggie so I could see what this new boy toy looked like.

"Why does it seem like you're being entirely honest with me?" I asked.

"Because I really want your grandfather's soul. I need your cooperation to wrench it from his flesh, and because of how poorly humans have treated you, I know a monster behaving honestly is the best chance I have at convincing you to help me."

Shit, I thought. *He's right.*

It's amazing who a person abused by humans will side with after a month of torment. I felt like an ant who escaped an arachnid's web only to team up with a spider wasp to come back and kill it later.

"What exactly do you need me to do?" I asked.

Arsyn slowly pointed to my shadow. My eyes followed his finger to look at the little bat-like figure my shadow became when Becky named me her First. It sat against the wall, mirroring my position in the chair.

"Your aunt hasn't shown you this ability yet, probably because she doesn't want you smuggling booze, but as a vampire, your shadow is more than just a shape created in view of the light. Press hard enough against it, and you'll feel your hand sink into a cold space accessible only to you."

I had to see this for myself, so I stood up and walked over to the wall where my shadow awaited me.

There's no way, I thought. A glance back at the table showed me Arsyn hadn't moved a muscle.

I placed my fingers on the drywall, the cool plaster seeming ordinary to my eyes and touch. My shadow didn't move. My fingers traced over my form until they hovered on my chest — er, my shadow's chest.

Taking a deep breath, I pushed, feeling resistance in the wall. Nothing happened. The plaster under my touch didn't budge. Adding more pressure, I grunted.

I was one second from asking Arsyn if he was just playing a prank when my shadow inexplicably gave way. One moment, I was touching the surface of a rock, and the next, my fingers were sinking into mud — or maybe jelly.

Wherever my fingers went, Arsyn was right. It was cold, like, stepping out in the dead of winter with no gloves on. I didn't feel anything in the space except for frigid air, assuming there even was air in the place where my fingers ended up.

Pulling back, I found my fingers to be just fine. They weren't even chilled.

"Damn that was weird," I muttered.

Turning back to Arsyn, I raised an eyebrow, waiting for an explanation.

"Vampires are mysterious creatures, you know? You haven't even tapped into half of what you can do with your aunt's borrowed powers. Man alive, Becky doesn't even know everything she can do as a fully-turned vamp."

I pushed into the shadow a couple more times,

sinking my hand in deeper with each exploration. My fingers didn't meet any resistance inside.

"So what is this thing?" I asked.

Arsyn leaned back in his chair and put his feet on the table.

"That's your little pocket. Every vampire has one. Your magic makes a little space that only you can access. And the only way in is through your shadow."

"So it's my… Vamp of Holding," I muttered as the demon rolled his eyes.

When I was done playing with my shadow, I turned back to the demon and threw up my arms.

"Okay, so that's a neat trick. I'm sure it'll come in handy. But what does it have to do with taking Ebeneazar down?"

Arsyn walked over to my shadow.

"It'll be a tight fit for me, darling. I shouldn't have eaten so much pasta with Tobey last night. Your shadow doesn't have as much space as Becky's. But I want you to stuff me inside like an oversized back-pack in your locker. Then, when you see your grandfather again, and believe me, the day is soon coming, I'll finally be close enough to grab him by the throat and claim my prize."

Glancing at my shadow and then to the demon once more, I asked, "Are you going to be okay in there?"

"Kitten, your concern for me is adorable. But

worry not. Compared to Hell, it'll be like taking a nap in a cozy sleeping bag."

Slowly nodding, I rubbed my chin.

"I guess that works," I muttered.

Arsyn flashed me a giant smile.

"Excellent. So… have you figured out what you want in exchange for helping me?" Arsyn said.

I sighed. Of course, we were back on this again. No, I hadn't been able to decide. Most folks spend their lives dreaming of getting three wishes from a djinn. And they imagine knowing exactly what they'd ask for. But I didn't have a clue.

The demon seemed to have expected this.

"I know you said I couldn't ask for a future favor. But what if we put safeguards on said favor?"

Arsyn raised an eyebrow.

"Safeguards?"

"What if you got… three vetos on any future favor you weren't capable of fulfilling?"

He seemed to consider this, squishing his lips to the side as variables and calculations raced through his mind like they probably had for millennia.

"Okay, darling. I can make that work."

"Great. So what happens now? You pull out a giant scroll for me to sign?"

A giggle erupted from the fruity demon's chest as he shook his head. Arsyn suddenly seemed in a good mood again.

"We'll keep this more simple," he said, cloak

parting so he could hand me what looked like a business card.

The paper was thick and textured like cardstock. A border of raised dots shaped like human skulls circled the entire thing. I read it aloud, white text on black paper.

"Vedalia Hardcastle agrees to assist Arsyn Fawnquin in his attempt to secure the soul of Ebeneazar Martin. For a period of no longer than 14 days, Vedalia will allow Arsyn to reside in her Vamp of Holding on the assumption that Ebeneazar will appear before her, at which point, Arsyn shall rise from hiding and claim what he is owed. In exchange, Arsyn owes Vedalia a future favor to be claimed within a decade. The demon is allowed up to three vetos on any favor he cannot or will not fulfill. Favor void if not claimed within 10 years."

I flipped the card over to find a blank line on the back where I imagined I needed to sign my name.

"Hardcastle is Aunt Becky's last name," I said. "She took it from Aunt Jazmine when they got married."

Arsyn nodded before saying, "And now their name is yours, is it not, kitten? They've made you their daughter, after all, further severing your relationship with Ebeneazar's side of the family."

My heart fluttered at hearing this. It's true. In the last month, they'd fudged some paperwork to adopt me after asking if that was what I wanted. But until I saw it in print as my identity in this binding document, it hadn't hit home.

"They made me theirs," I muttered, trying not to tear up in front of the demon.

Flipping the card over again, I re-read the text.

"Why keep this so short?" I asked. "The scroll you showed me when we first met was huge."

Arsyn produced a quill dipped in ink from beneath his cloak, and I was starting to wonder if he had his own Vamp of Holding with as many things as the demon brought forth.

"I figured keeping this as simple as possible would further help earn your trust. I truly do just want that damn soul. Nothing else. You're just a vehicle to get it, darling."

Taking the quill and signing, I felt the little card dissolve into ash. In a matter of seconds, it'd fallen through my fingers and vanished. Then suddenly, Arsyn had it in his hands again, pulling it beneath the cloak.

"Now, then. If you'd be so kind as to show me to my new quarters," he said, grinning.

Shrugging, I grabbed the demon and pushed him gently toward my shadow. When I pressed him up against the wall, Arsyn stopped.

"Look, I survived being cast down from Heaven like lightning and cratering into the fiery underworld, kitten. You can get a little bit rough, and I'll be fine."

Part of this was awkward because he was a foot taller than me. Blowing my hair from my face and summoning extra strength to my grasp, I shoved that twink into my shadow and watched him vanish like a stick being swallowed in quicksand.

I didn't feel any different with him in my Vamp of Holding. I expected to seem colder or stuffed. Neither happened.

"You… good in there, buddy?" I asked the empty room, awkwardly.

His hand shot out and flashed me a thumbs up, which I considered a good sign. Of course, that didn't stop the visual from being unnerving. Having something stick out of your shadow is fucking weird. And THAT made me shiver.

Not long after, I woke up to the feeling of a goddamn tiger covering half my body. With bedmates like Cymera, I wouldn't need a comforter even through the worst Maine winter.

"Okay, girl. I'm gonna need you to get all 300 pounds of your furry self off so I can piss," I muttered, looking out the window. The sun appeared to be well on its way to setting.

Shit, what time is it? I thought.

Cymera took her sweet time getting up, stretching, sticking her tongue out at me, and then finally letting me up. That cat and everything trapped under her moved on an entirely different clock called Tiger Time. She didn't care that my bladder was close to bursting.

Darting into the bathroom, I watched her paw downstairs, likely to alert Aunt Jazmine I was awake.

When I finally came downstairs and parked my butt at the kitchen table, Jazmine was busy going through a stack of papers.

"Hey, baby. You feel better after yesterday?" she wrote on a notepad, sliding it over to me.

I nodded.

"Thanks for letting me stay home from school today," I yawned, stretching.

My eyes spotted something wrapped in brown paper, and I signed, "What is that?"

Aunt Jazmine just smiled and slid it over to me.

"What, no hints?" I asked.

She shrugged.

It felt sturdy, whatever was in the package. And it was about the size of a sheet of paper. Unwrapping it, I found a canvas waiting for me.

"A painting?" I asked, flipping it over to reveal an image of me and Aggie dancing at the bottom of the sea in a large bubble. Glowing seahorses lit the sand we spun on. She'd painted us with a bunch of purple and blue hues highlighted by the soft, golden light of seven seahorses.

My eyes widened as a small index card spilled out of the package and onto the floor. I picked it up and read it.

"Val, will you go to the Snowflake Ball with me?" Aggie had written with a blue glitter pen.

I set the painting down and stared at it, covering my mouth in awe and trying to hide a smile so big that it threatened to snap my lips in two.

Aunt Jazmine put away her papers, got up, and kissed me on the forehead. Then she put on a coat and grabbed her car keys.

"Where are you going?" I asked.

She walked back over and grabbed the notepad, writing, "Got a volunteer shift at the blood bank tonight working security. I'll be back before Aunt Becky goes to sleep."

As she started toward the front door, Becky exited the bedroom, scratching herself and yawning.

They shared a kiss, and Jazmine signed something I didn't catch.

"I'm going dress shopping?" Aunt Becky spoke aloud as she signed. She seemed utterly confused. And, to be fair, she'd just woke up.

Jazmine pointed to me. Then she blew me a kiss and went outside.

Becky scratched herself again and then walked into the kitchen, eyeing my painting.

"Aw, that's adorable. My little gay niece got her first invitation to the Snowflake Ball."

Panic suddenly hit me as Aunt Jazmine's words from earlier sunk in.

"Aunt Becky! I don't have a dress to wear! And the dance is in a week."

She gestured for me to take a deep breath and chuckled.

"That's what my lovely wife was saying before she left. Apparently, I'm taking you to pick out a dress tonight. So much for watching British people bake pastries," she said, getting a coffee mug out of the cabinet.

I took a deep breath and looked at the painting again, trying to picture what kind of gown Aggie would wear. My mind quickly ventured to what she'd look like under the gown, and I immediately shook my head and cleared my throat.

"Want to order a pizza for dinner?"

"Or five?" I asked.

"That's my girl," Becky grinned, pulling out her phone as the coffee maker started up.

Looking at my dimly outlined shadow against the kitchen wall, I was suddenly reminded of my dream. I tried to picture Arsyn squished inside my Vamp of Holding and stifled a giggle.

"Hey, Aunt Becky?"

"Yeah?" she asked, watching the coffee pour into her mug.

"What do you know about demons?"

CHAPTER 17

A chilly sea breeze had enveloped the peninsula when Becky and I left the house and started toward the dress shop. I shivered a little bit and tightened the belt on my coat, trying to hold in any warmth that might have been otherwise escaping.

Becky took the lead as we turned onto Congress Street. She assured me the shop wasn't far, just back toward downtown.

It still blew my mind that I could walk almost anywhere I wanted in Portland. You couldn't do that in most Arkansas towns. Having a car or truck was a way of life. You got your permit at 14, your license at 16, and off you went. Public transit? Maybe if you lived in Fayetteville or Little Rock. You might have a bus stop accessible during daylight hours. But here? I could walk to Aggie's house, get coffee, grab lunch at a nearby Thai or Vietnamese restaurant, and just about anywhere else. I loved that.

"So. . . his name is Arsyn?" Becky asked as we walked past Aggie's bodega. I resisted the urge to turn my neck and see if she was working.

"Yes. And Ebeneazar scammed him and a bunch of other demons out of his soul."

My aunt cocked her head to the side and thought for a moment.

"I wish you'd told me about him before agreeing to this bargain," she started. "I'm not going to scold you because I'm not your mother, but. . . you have to be more careful with this demon business."

That stopped me.

Becky paused a couple of steps later and looked back at me.

"What's wrong, Val?"

I stared at the ground, trying to find the words I wanted to say. The vampire's phrasing had upset me, but it wasn't her fault. She was just spitting facts. Becky hadn't given birth to me, so she could hardly claim to be my mom. But still. . . I couldn't explain the tightness in my throat and the water building in my eyes without accepting a basic truth. I wanted Becky to be my mother. I did wish she'd given birth to me instead of the noncommittal woman whose egg I'd formed from.

And, universally speaking, I got pretty damn close, right? Becky was my mother's sister. It was like the universe had lined up the shot and then missed by a hair.

How did one communicate "I wish you were my mom" without it sounding cringe or embarrassing? If I said that, would she immediately kick me out of her house? No, that was just my brain playing mean tricks, right? Had to be. Just one of the fun joys of being an awkward teen girl. Sometimes your brain is your worst enemy. But sometimes, if you're lucky, your brain is only your second-worst enemy. Gotta give credit to a uterus that decides to turn my reproductive system into ravioli every month for not playing Baby Factory.

Wait. . . this is stupid. Just tell her, I thought. *She's already adopted you on paper. Just say the words.*

"Becky, you could be my mom, if you wanted. God knows your sister wasn't great at the job. There were nights after dinner when I couldn't get her to say two words to me. But in the month since I've been here, you've done a pretty kickass job."

She raised an eyebrow.

"Val, you don't have to say that to make me feel better."

I took a step toward her and felt words clog my throat.

"It's not about making you feel better! I spent my entire childhood not knowing what 'better' felt like. But you! You rescued me at my lowest point and gave me a home. You carried me through the trauma, you empowered me to feel safe, and dammit, those are the things a mother does. So, if you want to be my mom, then be her. I don't want to call anyone else that word except for Jazmine."

For a moment, I watched her face go through a flash of emotions, confusion, uncertainty, and joy. And then she snatched me faster than my eyes could see. I had two seat belts powered by vampiric strength wrapped around me.

"Mom!" I gagged from the hug of death, but being called that just made her squeeze me tighter. "Please, I'm dying, and I don't know how strong the healing powers I've pulled from you are."

Just before my face turned purple, the vampire cut me loose, and I spent the next minute dramatically breathing in and out.

"Well that was an embarrassing display," I huffed.

She leaned down and made a big show of loudly kissing my forehead. An unhoused man sitting under a nearby awning chimed in.

"Aw, that's so sweet! There's nothing more beautiful than a mommy doting on her baby girl," he said, clasping his hands together and twinkling his eyelashes at us.

Heat rushed to my cheeks, and I immediately regretted everything I said. People walking by us snickered as Becky said, "My sweet baby girl."

She'd gone from hesitating as I called her

"mother" to owning the role with nothing less than vamp speed, and I hated it.

Making a big show of wiping my forehead with my coat sleeve, I was mortified to realize she was wearing dark red lipstick.

"Mom!" I screamed. "That kiss is gonna leave a mark."

Running over to a bookstore closed for the night, I stood in the window and stared at my reflection. Plastered in the middle of my forehead was a slightly smudged kiss imprint.

Rubbing it with my coat sleeve wasn't doing much, and I suddenly felt flushed and even more embarrassed.

"I am NOT going dress shopping with this on my forehead!" I shouted.

Becky rolled her eyes and walked over. She stared at me for a moment and reached into her purse, pulling out a tissue. Licking it a few times, my new mother used the dampened end to wipe off her kiss.

"Oh, stop being overdramatic. Mothers kiss their daughters on the head all the time."

"Is that your saliva you're wiping on top of my face? Yuck! I've changed my mind. From now on, only Jazmine is my mother. Gross!"

While I gagged, she finished cleaning off the lipstick stain and tossed the tissue into a nearby trash can. Then, Becky took out a couple of dollars and tossed them into the unhoused man's cup.

"Thank you for helping me embarrass my daughter," she said, winking.

He gave her a mock salute.

"Mooooommmm!" I scolded, but she ignored me.

We finally started moving again, and she looked back in my direction.

"You're grounded, by the way," she started.

I scoffed.

"For what?"

"Striking a bargain with someone from the fiery pits of Hell without first asking permission. That could have cost you your soul, young lady! Demons are like people, okay? There are some benevolent spirits, and there are some assholes. But at the end of the day, most demons are simply bastards. They're bastard-coated bastards with bastard filling inside. And the next time I catch you striking a bargain with one before asking permission, I'll invite Agatha over for dinner and embarrass you so badly that she dumps your ass out of pity."

My face froze in an expression of utter disbelief. What had happened in the last 90 seconds for our dynamic to shift this rapidly? A few flowery words, and suddenly, I'd been adopted by a drill sergeant.

"Unbelievable! I thought you were the fun aunt. You sink boats in the harbor and mesmerize loud customers at Waffle Hut. How are you the one to ground me now?"

She looked at me with a smirk and all the authority and newfound power of a mother. And Becky was enjoying herself. It was as though being a mom gave her more power than being a member of the living dead.

"What you've just so astutely observed is a transition from fun aunt to responsible mother. Aunts get to feed their nieces soda and cake until they're about to puke. Then, they can toss the child at their mother and run away. You know who gets to clean up the vomit? The mom."

I shook my head, utterly unable to make sense of even half of what she'd just said.

"What does any of that have to do with you not being the fun aunt anymore?"

Becky opened her mouth to speak, but no words came out. Then she scratched her head and sighed.

"I need to read one of those parenting books Jazmine suggested," she mumbled.

I turned to look at her with wide eyes.

"Jazmine bought parenting books?"

The vampire smiled, eyes beaming with pride in her wife. It was a knowing look she'd flashed many times through their years together.

"Oh yes," she said as a motorcycle went roaring by us, forcing me to cover my ears and resist the temptation to vamp speed a stick through its tires.

"She bought three parenting books and read them all right after I left to find you. And since you've gotten settled, Jazmine has finished at least seven more books on parenting, including two on raising a gay child."

We walked in silence for a few blocks, passing Lincoln Park and coming into view of Portland City Hall.

A couple of seagulls called loudly to the city below that this was their nesting grounds, and we only lived here by their grace and mercy. The scary thing about these birds was their lack of fear. People, bikes, cars, trucks, vampires, nothing put the fear of god in these birds. And that terrified me. I'd watched one kill a pigeon and then eat it. I'd seen seagulls bigger than my head knock over a garbage can and enjoy their spoils.

Maybe I don't need Arsyn to take care of Ebeneazar, I thought, watching the birds glide overhead and shit on a police officer taking his dinner break. *Perhaps a few well-placed seagulls would scare him straight.*

After a couple of turns and walking through a tiny alley, Becky guided me to a little store called Emma's Bowtique. The store had a large glass window with two mannequins posed like they were about to dance. One wore a black and silver tuxedo while the other was clad in a strapless red dress that matched Mom's lipstick.

"I've heard good things about this place from a friend," Becky said, holding the door open for me.

Inside, a woman who appeared to be in her late 40s stood behind the register, checking out a mother and her son who were renting a tux.

When she was finished, and they left, the woman came over to Becky and me. Her hair was dyed blonde, and she had it styled into a manageable cut, bangs pulled back with a silver clip.

"Hi there, my name is Emma. How can I help you two?" she asked, crossing her arms. These were arms that would be as white as mine were it not for a tanning bed she probably had in her attic or basement.

Her tired smile said, "I close in an hour, and then I have a bottle of wine waiting for me, but I don't want my customers to know that."

Fair. Customer service can be a bitch, I thought.

"My daughter is looking for a dress for her first Snowflake Ball. And we'd love to see what you have available," Becky said.

Emma's blue eyes turned to me, and I. . . didn't like what I saw on her face. Maybe this was just another case of my brain being my worst enemy. Like when a friend takes more than 30 seconds to text you back, and suddenly, you're paranoid that they've started to secretly hate you.

But Emma looking me up and down felt less like someone trying to determine my color and style and more like she was ready to wrap me like a mummy with measuring tape. I didn't see someone eager to help a girl find the perfect dress for her date. Instead, I witnessed a woman judging every flaw in my complexion and curve on my body.

Mom said nothing, standing there with a hand on my shoulder while Emma finished her appraisal of my apparently less-than-desirable form.

It was subtle. This was a woman who knew how to hide her judgment so customers would continue to buy her clothes, after all. But I caught it in the tightening of her lips and the slight narrowing of her eyes. Emma even appeared to be wrestling an eyebrow from rising.

In the end, Emma managed to stretch that customer service smile across her face, pink lipstick doing nothing to hide her distaste for me. Did Becky not see it?

"Well. . . do you know what your boyfriend is wearing to the dance? I could help coordinate colors," she offered.

I flinched. How did you assume this shit in 2023?

"I'm going with a girl, actually. And. . . no. She only asked me a few hours ago. I don't know what her gown is like or if she even has one yet."

Emma's face was suddenly dripping with mock pity.

"Oh, I'm so sorry, dear. But hey! You can still have fun going with a friend. I think the guys call that 'going stag,' right? So you and your little friend will be going doe?"

I tried not to grit my teeth as my blood pressure rose. Emma's heteronormative pity was enough to make me want to smash something.

"I'm going to the ball with my girlfriend," I said, somehow keeping that ever-thinning polite smile stretched across my face.

Maybe she's just old and doesn't know better, I thought.

But all hope of that vanished with Emma's smile. All that remained in its place was an expression that struggled to remain neutral.

Becky spoke up, cutting through the awkwardness.

"My daughter's favorite color is red, so maybe we could start there?" the vampire asked. I did a double-take at Mom. How did she know my favorite color? As far as I knew, I hadn't said anything about it.

Good detective work, I guess, I thought.

Emma turned toward the rear of her store.

Black tile stretched back about 30 feet with two areas surrounded by mirrors for trying on clothes. Dressing rooms lined the back wall, one marked for ladies and the other for men.

Racks of dresses and suits hung spread out across the little store. Warm lights highlighted certain outfits on mannequins, probably the more expensive ones.

Emma walked past me, and I turned to follow. She was about a head taller than me and skinny as a rail. I wondered if it was yoga or pilates. Zumba perhaps? Jazzarobics? I giggled imagining the store owner before me darting from side to side and doing a sudden spin, dancing like her life depended on it.

She turned around to face us, again giving me an uncomfortable analytical stare. I twitched under that stare and rubbed one of my arms.

"Let's see what we have, hm?" she said, masking a small sigh.

And thus began my montage of throwing on different dresses, none of which were red.

Emma handed me a couple of cocktail dresses, one yellow and one blue. Neither seemed to fit me just right, and I didn't like the way they felt.

But Mom somehow made it fun, telling me to spin and doing her best Edna Mode impressions.

"No, no darling. You need to show more ankle. Remember, your power comes from the boldness of your strut. Now strike forward! Imagine yourself waltzing into the chamber as all eyes take notice. Do you want to be a meek sheep or a roaring lioness? The lioness of course, dear!"

I giggled and tried on a black maxi dress that fit me fine, but wasn't something I could see myself in.

Eventually, Emma excused herself to answer a phone call back at the register.

"Yes? This is her. Uh-huh. No, tomorrow

morning should still be fine," she started as I tuned out the rest of her conversation.

My eyes randomly settled on a red strapless ball-gown with a sweetheart neckline. The skirt was all bunched up with ruffles, and it came with a large fabric rose that would sit on my shoulder.

"Whoa. . . real princess shit," I whispered, taking a step closer.

Becky followed my gaze and spotted the gown.

"Oh, that's wicked gorgeous, bub. You have to try it on," she said, picking it up off the rack.

I cleared my throat and looked at the ground.

"But that's not one she picked for me," I managed to choke out. "What if she knows I won't look good in it?"

My mother rolled her eyes and shook her head in Emma's direction.

"Fuck her. You don't wait for people to hand you things in life. If you know the path you want to walk, then walk it. If you spend your life waiting for people to hand you the things you want, then you'll probably never get them. Now take this dress into the fitting room, and don't come out until you're wearing it," Becky said, thrusting it into my arms.

Heat rushed to my cheeks, and I continued to stare at the ground before muttering, "Thanks, Mom."

I found the dress to be a complex maze of zippers and fabric that needed to be tucked in different spots. But, eventually, I was covered in a red ball gown.

"Princess shit," I muttered again, looking at myself in the smaller dressing room mirror. The smile wouldn't leave my face. So, I walked outside, and Becky's expression lit up like the Fourth of July.

"Ayuh, that's a great fit for you," she finally managed after finding the words.

I twirled a couple of times and actually enjoyed the girl I saw in the mirror. That was such a rarity when you grew up with an unsupportive mother. I'd ask her how she thought I looked now and again after I got a new shirt or a pair of jeans, and the most I could raise from her was a noncommittal "That's nice" or even a grunt.

But Becky was taking pictures and sending them off to Jazmine and a few friends. I was tempted to send one to Aggie but decided that I wanted the outfit to be a surprise.

Of course, the next surprise I had in store for me was Emma returning with a look of shock on her face.

"Oh, no dear."

And people think that words are painful? Sometimes the lack of words is even worse. The agony you can inflict with an expression, a three-word sentence, and a small gesture like flicking your wrist is surprisingly potent. Just like that, the girl in the mirror wasn't so sure of herself. It didn't matter that she'd just been adopted or had vampire abilities. This ordinary human lady had stripped her down to size in mere moments.

"That wasn't one I selected for you. And you don't have enough time before the ball to. . . make it fit," she said, one hand clasped over the other.

Gotta give credit to Ebeneazar, strange as it sounds, he never shamed my image. I was never ugly or overweight or disproportional in his eyes. He'd figured out it was what's on the inside that counts. And he took issue with the little gay heart beating in my chest that swooned when pretty girls accidentally bumped me in the hallway at school. Which was. . . still bad, but in a different way.

People will find all kinds of ways to let you down, I thought, taking smaller breaths as if Emma might change her mind if I didn't inflate my lungs so much.

And sure, the dress was a little snug, but I felt pretty in the fucking thing. Shouldn't that be what mattered? That I looked in the mirror while wearing this dress and felt like I could fight Godzilla?

"Perhaps I can find something more in line with your body type, dear," Emma said, motioning for me to take the dress off as I might accidentally stretch it out if the garment remained on my body for much longer.

That little gay heart in my chest had stopped beating. And I pictured it shriveled up like a raisin, veins swinging loose as it hung there.

I turned toward the dressing room but stopped when I felt Becky's hand on my shoulder.

Fire blazed inside her crimson eyes as the vampire viciously stepped toward sudden new prey. I watched Emma deflate before my mother's sudden change in demeanor.

"Fuck you, bitch," she barked as Emma visibly flinched. "My daughter has dealt with more shit in the past 60 days than you have in your entire life! And the fact that she can put on a nice dress and still manage to find a genuine smile while looking in the mirror is proof she's a hundred times stronger and more beautiful than you ever will be."

The vampire spit venom as she spoke, her words dripping with malice.

"I've seen decay up close, Emma, smelled death as it wafted from a corpse looking for a neck to strangle. And none of that comes close to the ugliness you carry inside."

Emma opened her mouth and yelped when Mom grabbed her blouse at the collar. I watched the vampire pull Emma right up close until they were at eye level.

"I have just three simple instructions for you, Emma."

The store owner barely managed a nod.

"First, you're going to give us this dress free of charge. Box it up. Throw in a matching pair of nice heels, size nine. Second, you're going to forget we came in here today and even delete your security footage for the last hour. Finally, and this is the most important. Are you listening, Emma?"

Her eyes were wide with compliance as she nodded a second time.

"Good. Spend the next three months eating tons of carbs. I want you to feel good about yourself until you no longer can," she hissed, thrusting the shop owner backward.

Emma shook her head for a moment as her vision seemed to clear. And then she waited for me to change back into my normal clothes.

Afterward, she boxed up the dress, and the shoes, and sent us on our way so she could order a pizza or two.

We walked home, Becky carrying the dress, and me carrying the shoes. I quietly thanked her for standing up for me, and the vampire sighed.

"Look, Val. I'm not a perfect person, and I'm not gonna be a perfect parent. I've made a lot of mistakes in my life, but I'm going to do right by you as a mother, I promise."

I smiled and took her hand, which seemed to surprise the vampire. Becky looked down at me with a somber expression. It slowly warmed into a tiny smile.

"You've only ever been someone who rescues me, Mom. Whether that's from Ebeneazar or bitchy store owners, the result remains the same. You come through for me," I said.

When we got to Lincoln Park, Becky navigated us over toward an old wooden bench with iron armrests that had seen better days. Before us, a large cement courthouse stood, illuminated by a few different streetlights.

We sat down, and Becky put the outfit aside, clasping her hands together.

"Val, I'm not joking about the mistakes I've made in my life. And I don't want you to brush them aside or give me a free pass."

I cocked my head to the side.

"What mistakes are you referring to, exactly?"

She took a deep breath and let it out slowly. I could almost feel the weight of what she was about to share, bearing down on her shoulders. And I wondered if it was only her vampire strength that allowed her to carry such a load.

"I should have pushed harder to be more involved in your life, bub. Your mother and I used to be much closer, but when she announced her marriage plans with your father, I was outraged. I felt like. . . she could've done so much better. I watched him closely and always thought he was controlling and oppressive. Maybe it wasn't overt, but it felt like he broke my sister in like a horse, and she was never the same after joining Ebeneazar's family."

We sat in silence for a moment before the vampire continued her story.

"I was living in Ohio at the time and not handling the separation from my sister very well. I was angry. I was stupid. And I was reckless. One night, I decided that I was going to drive down to Arkansas and give them both a piece of my mind. Like I was going to save my little sister. It was dumb and impulsive. I was driving too fast when a big storm hit the highway. Most drivers had the sense to pull off and wait out the rain, but not me. I sped ahead."

Unsure of what to do now, I put my hand on Becky's, which she seemed to appreciate. She patted my lap a couple of times with her other hand.

"What happened?" I asked, quietly.

She scoffed.

"I lost control of my car. . . struck a minivan and killed a little old lady by the name of Jan Eliston. She was a grandmother of four and on her way home with groceries."

I gasped at the revelation.

"Long story short. . . I went to prison. Was supposed to stay there for a few years, but that place was hard, Val. I'm not saying I didn't deserve to be punished for my sins, but man alive, those places are supposed to rehabilitate us, teach us to be better than the deeds that got us locked up in the first place."

Holy shit, I thought, my mind reeling with the

knowledge that Becky was both a killer and a convicted felon.

I didn't judge Mom for her mistakes, but hearing that you'd killed someone and then went to prison for it will make anyone pause to think.

Becky flinched as she told the next part of her story, and I saw her start to cry for the first time since we'd met.

"Val, the fucked up things they did to us in there. . . treating us worse than animals. I knew they weren't there to rehabilitate me. I'd just been stuffed in a meat locker so society didn't have to look at the lady who got a poor sweet grannie killed on the interstate."

I lacked the courage to ask what came next, so all I could do was squeeze Mom's hand and let her know I was still right there, an anchor point to the present as she swam through this tunnel of horrific memories.

"After about nine months in that hellhole, a new inmate was added to the population. She was quiet and bothered no one. Everyone in that living mausoleum somehow understood this woman was not to be fucked with. It was primal. I don't know what she found so interesting in me, but I drew her attention. Skipping a few gory parts, I met my first vampire behind bars. And over the next month, she offered to turn me.

"Deciding that my rehabilitation wasn't going to

happen in an Ohio state penitentiary, I died and came back to life as the monster you see now. We easily made our escape, mesmerized the right folks, and suddenly, I was a free woman.

"Now, I keep tabs on her grandkids, make sure they're safe and out of harm's way. Something bad peeks its head over the horizon and sets its sights on the Eliston kids, I step in to take care of it before they even know they're in danger. It's the only penitence I can offer going forward, short of showing up on their doorstep and offering them a stake to drive through my heart."

I didn't know what to say. Never in a million years did I picture this being how Becky was turned. In prison after a manslaughter trial? Mother of god.

Though. . . I can't imagine too many vampire-turning stories are gentle, easy tales full of laughter and joy. Vampires are, by their nature, monsters. Some kill people for food. Some kill people to protect their daughters. My Mom was the latter, and in the end, that's what allowed me to squeeze her hand again and give her a reassuring smile.

"If you're waiting for me to say I regret becoming your daughter, then you're going to be waiting a while," I said.

She looked over at me with shock in her puffy eyes. A stray tear ran down her cheek before she wiped it with another tissue from her purse.

"I appreciate you being honest with me. And I

understand that you're not perfect. But I'd never in a million years want a perfect mom. A perfect mom wouldn't know failure or how to keep her daughter from making the same mistakes she did. A perfect mom wouldn't kill cult members or force bitchy store owners to eat their weight in carbs for her daughter to feel better about herself. You're exactly the mother I've wanted my whole life and nothing you've just told me changes that," I said.

Becky wiped her nose and pulled me in for another neck-snapping hug before kissing me on the forehead.

"Oh, that's just great! More kissy marks on my face from my overly affectionate vampire mom. Give me a tissue so I can use my own spit to get the stain off," I snapped.

She kissed me twice more on the forehead, and I sat there scowling at a scowl-proof parent.

"I hate my life. I wish I was back in the basement being hypnotized by a cult member," I muttered, seething at the utter humiliation.

"No, you don't, my sweet daughter. You're thrilled to have an embarrassing mother like me, and nothing I've told you or done to you changes that," she teased, getting up from the bench without getting me a tissue.

"Mooooooooooom," I moaned, stomping after her.

We walked inside the house a few minutes later to find. . . a bizarre scene. Jazmine was wrapping a cut on her arm, Cymera was licking blood from her paw, and a dead man wearing a vest with several knives lay on the floor sporting a large slash down the side of his skull.

Everyone froze as the door closed behind us.

"Who the fuck is this?" I asked as Jazmine pulled out her phone.

In her notes app, my ink witch mother typed, "Why are there kissy marks all over your forehead?"

With a deep sigh, I stomped upstairs to grab a wipe from my makeup removal kit. When I came back down, Becky was wrapping the wound and kissing her wife on the cheek.

Jazmine showed me her phone again, and she'd typed, "We're being watched."

The vampire vanished, along with the corpse, and reappeared a few minutes later.

"What did you do?" I stammered as she shut the door, coming back into the house with bloodstains on her jacket.

"Same thing we did with the hunter your girlfriend killed. . . tossed the body in the harbor," Becky said.

I shook my head like this was somehow supposed to be normal behavior. I guess it was in a monster household.

"What if someone finds the body?" I asked.

"Then they conclude it was killed by the claws of a big cat and start searching for escapees from the tiny zoo down in York," Becky shrugged as if this was no big deal. How many bodies had she hidden in Portland's harbor?

Before I could ask her that, she cracked her knuckles.

"Alright. Looks like Ebeneazar is getting impatient for your return to Arkansas. So maybe it's time we set a trap," Becky said.

Jazmine nodded while I raised an eyebrow.

"What exactly did you have in mind?" I asked.

My moms just grinned, and Becky said, "Pack your bags. We're goin' up to camp."

CHAPTER 18

"Are you sure they're going to follow us?" I asked, sitting on the cabin's porch steps. Moss covered part of the wooden railing I leaned on.

Sunlight filtered down through the trees as I stared out at Sebago Lake. It felt like we were miles from civilization, down a dirt road, which led to a gravel path and a two-mile hiking trail. A decently-maintained cabin had greeted us as we stepped into a clearing on the northwest side of the lake.

Jazmine, my only conscious mother at the moment, watched me closely as I scooted to the middle of the stairs to hide from the midday sun. Staying in the shade of a nearby oak tree, I stretched and cursed the giant fireball in the sky for my headache.

Sitting down next to me, Jazmine handed me her

phone. In the notes app, she'd typed, "They're already here."

Holding up her hand, the ink witch's eyes turned to gold. The hairs on my arms stood up, even under my jacket as I felt her magic expand across the porch and into the sky.

Only then did I catch a blue jay fluttering down from a nearby tree branch and onto her shoulder. The bird's blue, black, and white feathers shook in the breeze as it hopped up closer to Jazmine's lips. She lightly kissed the bird on the beak and held up a hand of various seeds and tiny nuts.

With her other hand, the ink witch typed on her phone.

"Meet Rey," she wrote.

I smiled as the blue jay's head twitched left and right, tiny black marble eyes glancing down at the chopped walnuts and almonds Jazmine offered.

"Hello Rey," I said, smiling, resisting the urge to reach up and stroke the animal's feathers. Fuck was that difficult.

If not friend, why friend-sized? I thought. *If not for petting, why so pretty and soft?*

"So what? You're a Disney princess now?" I asked, raising an eyebrow with a smirk.

The ink witch rolled her eyes and put her phone down. She moved her lips in a silent language. Rey left her hand and fluttered up to Jazmine's shoulder again.

I got the feeling she wanted me to watch closely, so I did. When Jazmine closed one eye, that same eye on Rey gradually changed colors. My jaw dropped as the blue jay stared at me with different colored eyes, one black, one solid gold.

"No way," I whispered. "You can see what Rey sees?"

Mom nodded and pulled her sweater down, exposing her bare shoulder. I watched Rey hop and scoot over her blue bra strap and then lean against the witch's skin. Another wave of magic washed over the staircase as Jazmine gently placed her hand over the blue jay. It felt like static as you pulled a fuzzy shirt from the dryer.

Before my eyes, Jazmine pressed down on the bird, and where I expected to hear a shriek of protest, Rey remained silent.

After a couple of seconds, the ink witch's hand lay flat against her shoulder. When Jazmine moved her fingers, I spotted Rey flat against her umber skin, a vibrant, colorful tattoo once more.

"Am I going to see what other tattoos you have on your body one day?" I asked.

Jazmine silently chuckled and ruffled my hair before letting her locs down.

I looked out over the clearing that led down to the lake, gray water rippling in the afternoon breeze. Back in Arkansas, it was probably in the 50s or 60s today. But even with all this sunlight, Maine wasn't going to top 40.

Someday I'll get used to the cold, I thought, looking back at the cabin again. It had two bedrooms and no electricity. On the far end of the porch stood an old pile of firewood under a partially raised blue tarp. We'd started pulling out logs when we arrived last night and got a fire going in the wood stove.

My shivering ass was initially skeptical after our frigid hike, but after half an hour or so, I'd stripped down to my pajamas and was plenty warm.

We'd kept things simple last night. Becky cooked a pot of stew over an open fire behind the cabin and a skillet of instant mashed potatoes.

Granola bars and sandwiches had kept me going through most of today, but Becky promised to make a big supper once the sun went down.

I checked my phone and made a mental timer. She'd be up in four hours.

Turning back to Jazmine, I cocked my head to the side.

"How many did Rey — sorry, you — see?"

"Five hunters. No sign of your grandfather," she wrote in her notes app.

My heart skipped a beat. Five? Mother of god that was a lot of people. When hunters had gotten the jump on me or Becky before, it'd just been one man. And now my grandfather had called five fresh hunters to bring me in.

"Motherfucker," I sighed, hand over my eyes and dragging down my face. "You're a witch. Can't you just memory-wipe him or something?"

Jazmine patted me on the back and typed out, "Not that kind of witch."

We sat there on the porch for another half hour. I leaned my head on her shoulder and took in her smell. Mom typically wore a vanilla lotion and had the natural scent of paper and tea leaves underneath.

"You know, Mom, it's strange to think we've set a trap. This doesn't feel like setting a trap. It feels like a weekend outing for the fam. That's not something I got much of back in Arkansas. What did y'all call it? Making camp?"

Jazmine typed, "Going up to camp. It's a Maine thing."

I chuckled at that. I was picking up a few different Mainerisms.

"Maybe we can come back here when it's all over? When we're just two moms and a daughter instead of targets for a goddamn cult?"

My eyes unfocused for a moment as I imagined various holidays spent here at the cabin, the Labor Days, Four of Julys, camping trips, and more. Becky would grill supper, and we'd eat outside on the porch looking up at the starry night sky. Jazmine would teach me to fish in the lake, and we'd plant a summer garden here, maybe grow some wild blueberries. Perhaps we'd pick them and make home-made blueberry ice cream.

Lazily drifting off, I rested my head a little harder against Jazmine's shoulder, dreaming of that ice cream we'd all make together.

In my mind, summer fireflies danced between the trees, tiny lights needling the darkness back with a soft glow for a few seconds at a time. Braver bugs hovered closer to the water where a smallmouth bass might leap up and snatch them.

We hung a little wooden swing from a nearby tree that I could use to shoot out even further into the lake with a jump fueled by vamp strength.

All of those images were the future I wanted, the one I'd fight for. And the fight came far sooner than any of us wanted.

Jazmine's hand shook my shoulder with a gentle, yet urgent message. "They're here."

Standing up and fighting a yawn, I spotted a man in camouflage pants and a green vest standing by the lake, arms crossed. A rifle was slung behind him with a brown strap.

His glasses reflected a lower afternoon sun. How long had I been asleep? An hour? It was still too early for Becky to wake up.

The bald man took a few steps closer, his eggshell hands reaching into his pockets.

"I just want to say for the record... that normally I'd have no qualms about killing you, witch. But it's cold, and I want to head back to my truck. Walk the girl down to me, and I'll leave you and the bloodsucker in your cabin alone. It's a three-day drive back to Arkansas, and I'd like to get this over with."

His voice was the personification of gravel. I looked over at Jazmine, her face resolute and defiant. She'd faced hunters before and always walked away the victor. Today would be no different. Nobody was taking her new daughter.

I found a rock the size of my palm. It was a beefy little chunk of granite that whistled in the wind after I hurled it at the hunter. Vamp vision was great because I got to see the thing soar toward the lake and smash into the hunter's head, cracking into three pieces and shattering his glasses into many more.

His skull took the full brunt of the force my arm had tossed at him with vamp strength. I watched his head whip backward in a splurt of blood from a broken nose. His torso soon followed, stumbling in reverse until he fell into the water, spots of faded red floating to the surface. The hunter did not immediately rise from the water.

My mouth said, "First shot fired, you fucker."

My brain was full of screams and raw nerves as an inner voice hollered for Ebeneazar's men to just leave us the hell alone.

But they didn't seem inclined to do that.

Four more men stepped out of the trees with

rifles and shotguns pointed in our direction. They didn't look all that different than their buddy I'd smoked with a rock.

"Scatter!" I yelled, and dove for the pile of firewood as the first gunshots rang out. Mom ran into the cabin and pressed her back flat against a wall, yanking her sweater off.

Gunshots that might as well have been cannon fire tore the front porch apart, splinters flying in every direction. My ears rang, and I cursed the fact that I had enhanced hearing as I did every time a firetruck or ambulance drove by with the sirens blaring.

Putting that all aside, I kicked an opening in the porch rail, squeezed through, and darted into the tree line. None of them seemed to notice me. So when I came at their group's rear with a hollow log and smashed it over the head of one hunter, they were a little surprised.

I pulled part of the wooden porch railing I'd smashed out from behind me and shoved the whole thing through another hunter's knee. He went down screaming.

My victory was shortlived as the nearest hunter, a man with pierced ears and a forehead tattoo of a dragon nailed me in the cheek with the butt of his rifle.

Hitting the ground hard, I gasped and crouched, pain radiating through my entire head.

He stood over me with the rifle pointed at my shoulder and hissed, "Give me a reason, you little bitch."

"She's coming out of the house!" another hunter called with a higher voice than I expected.

All attention turned toward the cabin entrance as Jazmine emerged, eyes glowing gold. And I swear to god, the remaining hunters gasped in damn-near unison at what we witnessed.

"Tell me that's not real," a hunter said.

"Is that a fucking dinosaur?!" the man over me yelled.

My aunt let out a tight hiss with her tongue, and the creature rose from behind her, emerging from the shadows of the cabin.

The hunters didn't get a chance to respond as a feathered raptor bigger than any man present raced across the clearing. Short white feathers covered its head and neck while the torso was spattered in denser brown feathers. The raptor's tail had the darkest plume that widened out a little like a beaver's tail.

Long and narrow feathers in a gradient of brown and white extended from the back of its arms. Razor-sharp claws hung down from the raptor's hands and stood atop the raised toes of each foot.

The motherfucking dinosaur darted left toward me after Jazmine gave a sharp whistle between her thumb and index finger. I watched the man above me raise his rifle in panic and yell something unintelligible.

He got off a wild shot that hit the porch, and then the Utah raptor's snout tore into his throat, blood splattering all over its gray scales.

With a gurgled choking noise the tattooed man fell backward, eyes wide with disbelief. The raptor made quick work of the rest.

Jazmine crossed the clearing and helped me to my feet.

"How did you bring a dinosaur to life?!" I hissed, watching the raptor licking blood from one of its claws. Its yellow eyes glanced over at us now and again.

Mom just gave me a coy grin and offered no explanation. Up until now, I was under the impression she'd captured these live creatures into tattoos. But now I wasn't so sure. Unless she'd gone back in time 130 million years to find one.

That'd be ridiculous, right? I thought. *Right?*

My focus was shattered by another gunshot that clipped a branch just above Jazmine's head. It was followed by the sound of a boat engine racing across the lake in our direction. My eyes honed in on the craft and spotted at least 10 more guys.

Adrenaline raced through me anew as I started to consider flight for the first time instead of fighting. Where did my grandfather keep finding hunters to send our way? Was there a Hunters R Us store I didn't know about?

Unlike the ragtag group we'd dispatched, I spotted matching uniforms here. All black. Protective vests and helmets. Long guns. These assholes weren't fucking around.

"Mom?" I gasped before she tackled me to the ground behind a tree. Another gunshot struck a rock near us, sending pieces of granite everywhere.

The boat would be on us in a minute or less, and all my hammering heart wanted to do was run. Fight over. We lost. Let's get the fuck out of Dodge.

But that wouldn't solve anything, I realized. The vamp in black fled across the country, and the cultist followed. He just could not be reasoned with or convinced to leave well enough alone. It was like Arsyn had said. I was egg on his face, an embarrassment he let slip through his fingers.

But a fucking monster-slaying squad? That was overkill!

Mom didn't seem to be picturing the same strategy as me. She stood behind the massive ash tree we'd fallen behind as another gunshot clipped the trunk. Only now did I notice her tattoos with the sweater removed. Cymera covered one arm. A ball of fire was painted under her breasts. Opposite of Cymera on the other arm I spotted a night sky complete with stars and a full moon just below the crook in her arm.

Her face covered in sweat, Jazmine stood and raised the arm of stars. My eyes widened as she gritted her teeth, eyes glowing brighter than ever before. Then her sweat turned to drops of gold as well. Magic didn't just race over us. It poured out through the woods and into the sky as Mom's fingers traced over the tattoo of stars.

One by one they vanished beneath her touch, and I watched in disbelief as the sky above us darkened.

"An eclipse? Now?" I muttered.

But that wasn't it at all. The ink witch kept her arm raised high, ink shooting up in massive globs accompanied by gold light.

"Mom?" I asked, but she just gritted her teeth and kept going, palm tracing up her arm.

Looking up, I watched her ink swallow the clouds and every ounce of sunlight. When the moon vanished from her arm, a pale light took its place in the sky, the familiar silver orb glaring down at invaders attacking our cabin.

"No way," I whispered. "No way."

And then… it was night. The daylight was all gone. My phone said it was 1:30 p.m., and it felt like fucking midnight.

My eyes adjusted to the lack of light with little issue.

Without warning, the boat crashed into the shore. I heard a scream as the Utah raptor smoked one of the hunters, followed by more gunfire. The dinosaur hissed, and suddenly, Jazmine slumped against the tree. Her heart was racing, breathing ragged. I wondered if she'd ever used this much magic before.

"Mom?" was all I had to say before one of the hunters appeared with a gun pointed at us.

"Lights out," he said with a horrible sneer.

I watched his finger twitch just before hearing the sound of bones snap. And suddenly, he was on the ground in a heap of combat gear, head twisted entirely around.

Becky came into view where the hunter once stood, fangs glistening in the darkness. I watched a cruel and animalistic smile cross her face before she raised the limp body to drink.

A gunshot clipped her shoulder, and she barely flinched. As she drank and blood ran down her jaw, I watched her flesh mend itself with an unsettling squelching sound beneath her jacket.

When she was satisfied, exuding warmth, and eyes glowing a bright crimson, Mom dropped the body and looked down at her wife, extending a hand.

"Hey babe. Someone call for a massacre machine?" Becky said with a confident gleam in her smile.

"How did she do this?" I asked, feeling relief flood through my chest at our backup arriving mid-battle.

Becky winked.

"She's a badass witch," Mom said. "I'm gonna run her to shelter inside the cabin so she can catch her breath. Be right back."

The vampire vanished with Mom as more gunfire erupted in the night. I'm guessing these assholes weren't equipped with night vision goggles. They clearly attacked during the day hoping to avoid fighting a vampire.

True to her word, Mom reappeared at my side and threw her arms around me. I buried my face in her leather jacket.

She quickly whispered, "No mercy. We kill them, or they kill us, got that?"

I nodded.

"We'll deal with all the guilt and human bullshit later. Right now, you snap necks. I'll rip out hearts and tear off arms. Grab with both hands and twist with all your might. Give 'em the owl treatment, bub."

Again, I nodded, numb to all the emotions now rushing through my chest. Adrenaline was a hell of a drug.

With a bullet blowing right through her guts, I heard Becky snarl and then vanish into the darkness. A few seconds later, there was more gunfire followed by a scream.

I took a deep breath and darted into the fray, remembering what Mom had said.

Grab. Twist. Grab. Twist. Grab. Twist, I thought to

myself over and over, as if that'd make the action any easier.

Killing my first hunter was as miserable an experience as taking out the man in Indiana.

Turning, I saw two of the hunters unload entire clips on the raptor, and the creature exploded into a massive puddle of ink. Before my eyes, the murky puddle raced across the ground and toward the cabin.

"That's not good," I muttered, taking out another hunter.

Becky and I continued taking them down darting between trees. By my third kill, I had a hunter's corpse in my arms, taking long breaths, trying to keep my heart from exploding.

Don't think about it, Val. Just keep going, I thought.

But questions erupted in my mind. Did this man have a family? Had he fired his gun at us, or was he just here for backup? Was I a killer if I took lives in self-defense?

"Val!" I heard Becky shout.

That was my first indication something was wrong.

Looking down, I noticed blood pooling under my jacket and pouring down my belly.

"What the fuck?" I gasped, noting a large hole in my chest right where my heart should've been.

The forest started to spin, and my vision swam. Was I in the lake or still on the shore? Weakness flooded through me worse than I'd ever felt it, and I collapsed to my knees. Then my face was in the dirt, and darkness started to circle.

"I can't. . . feel it beating," I choked out before losing myself to an inescapable wave of shadow.

* * *

I CAME to sitting in a chair. Not a stiff chair. Not a comfy chair. A chair that was just serviceable enough not to hurt my tailbone. It was red. Damn thing almost swallowed me whole.

Looking up, I noted my surroundings were pretty sterile. White tile floor. An end table with a few magazines I didn't recognize. A tank full of tropical fish swimming between plastic pirate ships and skeletons.

Everything smelled of bleach and other cleaning chemicals.

To my left and right were two doors on opposite ends of the room. They appeared to be heavy. One was solid steel and the other was. . . bone? Its uneven alabaster surface even came with a handle shaped like a hand devoid of flesh.

"Well that's offputting," I muttered.

A window in front of me revealed an empty office with the computer turned off.

"Am I in a waiting room?" I asked nobody in particular.

The only noise filling the room was a gentle hum from the tank's pump.

My eyes darted from a potted fern to the doors again.

Walking over, I found the steel door frigid, cold to the touch. My breath fogged up when I stood close enough. There was no handle, so I tried pushing, and the damn thing wouldn't budge. It didn't even rattle. I might as well have thrown my weight against a brick wall.

"Okay. . . guess I'll try door number two," I mumbled, only to find I could neither pull nor push it open.

It was nearly scalding to lay hands on, and I started to sweat just being near it.

"Motherfucker, what am I supposed to do?" I yelled, wiping my forehead and stepping back from the door.

A familiar voice behind me spoke up.

"You wait, darling."

I turned to find Arsyn sitting in the large red chair I'd awoken in. His cloak was wrinkled, but his hood was down.

"Where are we? Another dream?" I asked him.

He patted the empty chair space next to him, and I cautiously reunited my ass with the red cushion. I was amazed the seat was big enough to comfortably fit us both. Only then did his gunmetal gray eyes lock with mine.

"No dream this time, kitten. You're in The Barren."

The demon didn't sound pleased. In fact, for the first time, I heard pity in his voice. Not an overwhelming amount, just enough to be noticeable.

"What is The Barren? Why does it look like a waiting room?" I asked, cocking my head to the side and fearing what answers would come. My leg started to shake uncontrollably.

Arsyn just sighed. But he didn't shy away from my questions.

"You're dead."

"Like. . . in a coma?"

"No. Dead."

"As in. . .?"

"Dead. Mortuus. Muerto." he said gently, but firm enough that I understood the finality of his tone. We weren't joking. We weren't beating around the bush. It was like the difference between how people down South talked and folks I'd met in Maine.

Southerners talk slow. I don't know if we know it or why, but we do. And so often we beat around the bush. There's almost a dance to the conversation in our heads. But the New Englanders I'd met thus far were very direct in their speech. Most of them liked to get right to it, no pussyfooting around. And it wasn't like they were mean. They just had a different way of speaking that I still wasn't used to.

I had more questions. Who wouldn't after being

told they're dead? But my eyes got a headstart and began to rain. And they rained. They rained like never before. Nothing had ever felt this dreary before, not being chained in that basement, not my Dad yelling at me for asking him a second time if he'd come to the Father/Daughter Breakfast in middle school, and not even killing a man in Indiana to save Becky. None of the murders I'd committed in the woods left such a stain on my heart.

So, yeah, the rain fell. What else could be done?

Arsyn waited patiently and only handed me a handkerchief from beneath his cloak. It smelled of sulfur and had a stag sewn into the corner.

"To borrow a quote from a favorite author of mine. . . you lived what anybody gets, Vedalia. You got a lifetime. No more. No less. You got a lifetime."

But there was so much more I wanted to do! How could this be it? A shot through the heart in a fight for my life. I hadn't even felt the fucking thing until it was too late. How could this be the end?

More rain.

And then Arsyn and I spoke anew after I'd drowned his poor handkerchief in my salty tears. The damn fabric square probably held an ocean at this point.

"So. . . what now? How long do we sit here?" I asked.

Arsyn shrugged.

"There's not really a 'long' here, nor a 'short.' The

Barren just is. It may be one of the only places where Time isn't welcome. A harbor no boat can reach."

I raised an eyebrow.

"Okay, so, what do we do?"

"We wait," he said. "That's what The Barren is for. It's a room to wait."

The demon crossed his legs, but his cloak still kept me from seeing the rest of his body. I sighed and looked around the nondescript room again. Where was the light in this place even coming from? I couldn't see outside. There were no bulbs or tubes on the ceiling. The place was just naturally bright as if the air itself held every ray and wave of light.

I crossed my legs and folded my hands without saying anything more.

"Now you're getting it, darling. Look, the truth is few people wind up in The Barren. You only show up here if there are. . . extenuating circumstances to your death. What we're waiting on is to determine if being Becky's First can restore your life. Or if the powers she granted you lack the potency to bring you back."

A tiny flutter of hope relit in my heart.

"I can go back?" I asked.

Arsyn shrugged again.

"It's. . . possible. I don't know enough about Firsts to determine for sure. But you took a bullet to the heart, not the head. I knew a wizard in Chicago who came back from that. Of course, his circumstances were even more bizarre than yours."

"Can we get back to me possibly rejoining the living?"

The demon raised a hand as if to caution me.

"Steady on, kitten. That's just one possibility. The other is you die and move along to the After. I'd say your odds for that are infinitely greater. It's the most common ending to every human's story."

I stared down at the tile floor, feeling that tiny flutter of hope waver like a candle on a breezy spring night.

"Okay, what are the possible outcomes here?" I asked.

Arsyn pointed at the doors.

"Eventually, one of those two doors will open. You don't get to choose which door or when. But it will happen all the same. One door returns you to that forest with your new moms and grandfather's men. The other door takes you to the After. Either way, there's no arguing."

Faces flashed before my mind. Jazmine, Becky, Aggie, Amelia, Dr. Dubois, I wasn't ready to say goodbye to any of them. I'd just gotten my new life.

Please don't take it away, I thought, closing my eyes for more rain.

With tears blurring my vision once more, I turned to the only person in the world I wanted at my side through this.

"Will you please wait with me?" I whimpered.

Arsyn's eyes narrowed, laced with pity once more.

"Of course, darling. I wouldn't think of leaving you alone here."

The demon's cloak parted briefly, and his hand took mine. His touch was cold, but welcome all the same. Because it told me one sure thing. No matter which door opened, I wasn't alone.

I closed my eyes after a while feeling the exhaustion of everything weighing on my very soul. And I found my head being guided over to a shoulder.

A familiar cloak rested under my cheek as we waited alone together, accompanied only by the music of one dedicated fish tank pump. Hey, there are worse ways to go out.

I heard the squeaking of hinges as a door eventually opened. My eyes were still shut tight, but I held onto Arsyn's hand for dear life.

"Steady on, kitten," he whispered.

And then the light swallowed me in one mighty gulp. Even with my eyes closed, all I saw was white. Scorching, blinding, white.

WITH A BOLT of lightning in my chest, I darted upward.

Everything was blurry for a moment until I heard

a quiet thump. Looking down, I saw a slug on the floor covered in blood. . . my blood.

Was that. . . in me? I thought, hazy on the details.

I was back in the cabin, and. . . my body had just pushed out the bullet that'd struck my heart and sent me to The Barren.

"I'm back," I gasped as sudden weakness wrecked my body again.

Falling helplessly toward the floor, I felt an arm catch me.

Staring up, I saw the face of one Ebeneazar, the cult leader, and my grandfather. His chilled blue eyes filled with some modicum of relief as breath entered my lungs once more.

He was the one who'd caught me.

"No. . .," I whispered, dread filling every single bit of space in my chest. I didn't return to life just to be greeted by this asshole, did I?

His white hair was combed neatly, and his button-down western shirt was a little wrinkled and stained with mud. Same for his jeans. But this was my grandfather alright.

"Thank the Lord," he said, closing his eyes in prayer. "My prayer brought you back to me."

Bullshit. My aunt's powers brought me back, I thought. But I didn't say that because my throat was paralyzed in fear. Someone had tied one of those twisty things used to seal a bag of bread around my vocal cords.

"Now I can take you back home and put this right once and for all," he said, opening his eyes again.

I shook my head.

"It's okay! I'm not mad, Vedalia. None of this was your fault. That vampire took you from me and mesmerized you to think you were part of her family. But that's all over now," he said as if he'd just given a closing statement in court, and the entire jury had bought it.

Looking to the right, I saw Becky and Jazmine sitting against the back wall, tears in their eyes, and hands over their mouths. They looked relieved. But the two men standing over them with guns seemed less than impressed.

My grandfather turned to those men.

"After I take the girl, kill them," he said. No malice. No hatred. The command was spoken like a dad telling his kid to rake the leaves or clean his room. And those words were given with the understanding that Ebeneazar's command would be followed without question.

"Mom," I gasped, looking at each of them, feeling fear and weakness holding me down like chains of finality.

Did I really leave The Barren to return to this? Would it have been better for me to move on to the After if Ebeneazar was waiting for me here?

I shuttered as these questions raced through my head.

Ebeneazar ran his other hand down my cheek, and I didn't even have the power left within me to bite it. His touch was oily and left me mentally squirming. But I could barely scowl. If using vampiric strength and speed left me weak. Then coming back to life from a fatal gunshot left me feeble.

My hands shook, and it was difficult to focus my eyes.

"Easy now, granddaughter. I'll get you back to the boat, and then you'll be home before you know it. I didn't want to fly up here, but those monsters pretending to be your family left me no choice. It's all over now, though."

Was it? Surely this couldn't be the end. And yet, I didn't foresee Aggie leaping to my rescue this time. Tears ran across my cheeks.

"No crying, now. You're safe. I'm going to take you home and bring you renewed joy and hope in the redeeming love of our savior. I will replace the lie these monsters gave you with the truth of the Word. This is a time to be jubilant, Vedalia. For my prodigal granddaughter has returned to me."

His words slid over my ears like cotton, and my mind wanted things to be as easy as he promised. But no! I wouldn't accept this false silver from him. I wouldn't allow his depraved dogma steal my future again!

What else can I do? I thought, my heartbeat turning more anemic by the second. I'm spent. My moms are spent. We're alone. My future is his again.

In between tears, I stared at the floor. Light from the wood stove cast a warm, orange glow through the room and chased away the cold and shadow from outside. It was night. My body had clearly taken hours to heal, and all the stars had returned to Jazmine's arm.

My eyes watched the rough, wooden floor for a few seconds more. Flickering light from the glass on the stove's load door cast our shadows in an inter-twined shape.

Ebeneazar's shadow and my own.

Looking up into his cold eyes again, I saw Ebeneazar's stern expression retake him. Being chained to a radiator for a month in a basement was far too lenient, his face said. When we got back to Harrison, the cult leader would find something worse for me in between brainwashing sessions.

My grandfather raised an eyebrow.

"Penny for your thoughts before we leave, grand-daughter?"

I took a deep breath, still shaking, and I managed to whisper, "I'm just now realizing that you have another smell under that Celtic Spring bar of soap you wash with religiously."

Ebeneazar looked confused and decided I must have been delirious. Death would do that to a girl.

"You smell like sulfur, Ebeneazar."

His eyes widened at that remark, and with the last of my strength, I shouted, "Arsyn! Take him now!"

A maniacal giggle erupted from my shadow beneath me, and two elongated arms made entirely of obsidian fire shot up and wrapped tightly around my grandfather.

He hissed as the frigid flames ate at a bit of his shirt and sleeves.

The arms raised Ebeneazar higher and higher until his back was pressed against the ceiling. Beneath my head, I felt a new hand that smelled of molten rock and sulfur. It was the hand that gripped mine patiently in The Barren and waited with me.

"Oh, darling. I'm so relieved to find this twist of events. I was worried you were heading for the After, and I was going to return here empty-handed."

Another giggle.

"But this is so much sweeter than I could ever have hoped. Hello, Ebbe. It's been a while. How have you been?"

"Arsyn? How are you here? I exorcised you years ago!" Ebeneazar managed to choke out as the fiery arms held him aloft.

"Oh, that's the thing about demons. We're remarkably hard to get rid of for long. While you've been yucking it up and scamming my contemporaries, I was busy climbing from the bottom of a damned inferno. I crawled through darkness. I bathed in liquid flame. I screamed until shrill noise was all that remained of my spirit. But one image kept me going, Ebbe. One hope. And it was this very moment."

Ebeneazar turned to me, panic in his eyes. I'd never seen him like this. His face was sweating, and his lips were thin, pressed tight.

Gunshots rang out as the two remaining hunters opened fire on the demon who'd ensnared their payday.

"Oh no no no, you naughty boys," the demon laughed, walking toward them. His cloak seemed to swallow every bullet. From beneath his garment, Arsyn produced a massive deer antler in each hand. He stabbed one into the chest of a hunter. Then he gouged the other through the remaining gunman's eye socket.

As the demon's antlers dripped with carmine blood, I watched Arsyn squish them into his skull until they stood bright and tall before us all.

Arsyn then dropped his cloak, revealing the toned upper body of a man and the lower half of a demented buck. His legs were tall and gangly, covered in bronze-colored fur right down to the onyx hooves clicking on the cabin floor.

Ebeneazar screamed at the sight of the demon,

and I once more felt an otherworldly chill at the drop of the cloak. It devoured every ounce of warmth in the room, and even Becky was shivering by this point.

My grandfather turned his eyes to me again and yelled, "Don't give me to him, Vedalia! I'm family. Real flesh and blood family, girl. I can tell you where your mommy and daddy are. I have their address. I'll convince them to take you back."

Even in the grip of a demon, my grandfather still found a way to make the hurt rocket into my chest again.

"Convince them. . . to take me back?" I hissed, sitting up.

The cult leader nodded.

"Well, of course. I can do it. Ain't a single person in this world I can't talk down. You know that."

Was more rain in the forecast? Probably. Was more Dr. Dubois in the forecast? Absolutely.

"When your father called me after you told him you were gay, he was tired. So tired. Your mom was too. Their marriage has never really been all that solid, and they thought a kid would fix it. Obviously, you didn't. But that's not your fault either. That's when I saw the chance to save your soul. So I paid your parents a small fortune to give you to me. They didn't even hesitate, granddaughter. Took the suitcase of cash, called a realtor, and moved out of state."

My heart shattered with every word he revealed.

This was the missing puzzle piece I'd never asked for. And as he mashed it into the frame, pounding the edges to fit, I wept for the assholes who brought me into the world and straddled me with the impossible task of fixing their relationship. Can you even imagine? A fetus who isn't a whole person yet, and I was already shackled with a mission. They put all their hopes and dreams of repairing a decrepit bridge on an unborn child instead of just going to therapy or getting a divorce.

Then again, neither of those things is really an option when you're in a cult.

"Vedalia?" Ebeneazar called from the ceiling.

I looked up at him one last time, tears running down my cheeks. How was I not dehydrated yet?

"If you let this abomination take me now, you'll be less than human. Call him off. Choose your family," he all but hissed.

So I found the will to somehow stand on the world's wobbliest legs and glared up at him.

"Fuck you, old man. I do choose my family. And my family is made of monsters. Over the last month, it was monsters who rescued me, monsters who put my heart back together, and monsters who gave me a future. I spent my entire life with humans who didn't feed me a table scrap of love. But since I got to Maine, I've been given adoration in abundance."

My grandfather scoffed, somehow still able to

display disgust in the face of damnation. It was almost impressive.

"So, fine, I'll be less than human. I'll be a monster, Ebbe. Because that makes me happy. Take him down, Arsyn. One-way ticket. Express line. No waiting," I growled.

The demon winked at me and said, "Right away, kitten. Come along, Ebbe. I've got some friends who have been waiting a long time to meet you."

With that, the arms and hands of blackened fire pulled a screaming old man toward the floorboards, through the floorboards, and beyond the floorboards, with a rush of steam and shadow, beyond this life and into the After this cult leader had committed himself to with a bargain decades ago.

I collapsed to my knees as Arsyn descended into the Earth, and my moms rushed over, throwing their arms around me.

We just sat there in each other's grip for the better part of half an hour before my stomach growled loud enough to wake sleeping turtles at the bottom of Sebago Lake.

"Can we go, please? And maybe hit a drive-thru on the way home?" I whispered.

Becky just laughed and said, "Anything you want, my sweet baby girl."

Jazmine kissed us both as exhaustion and hunger threatened to pull me to the ground again. But my moms held me up, just as they had for the last month and as they would continue to do for many years to come.

Soaring through the clouds, I watched the patchwork quilt of Earth several thousand feet beneath us. Turbulence rattled the plane, but Amelia held her steady. It was loud. . . so damn loud. You don't realize how quiet flying on a 747 is until you climb into a personal aircraft.

But I tucked that complaint behind my ear and looked at the console of switches and buttons.

"I still can't believe you can just fly us around like this," I said.

"Well, as long as Dad pays the fuel bill I can," Amelia giggled, looking at a few different gauges.

In the seat behind me, Aggie leaned forward and rested her chin on my shoulder.

"This is cool and all, Amelia. But what I really want to discuss is your date to the Snowflake Ball. You said a guy asked you?"

I gasped and looked at my bestie with anticipation. Short of killing hunters in the woods and dumping their bodies in the lake, this was the most exciting thing to happen to me in the last few days.

"Okay, don't judge me. I'm going with Markus Wayne," she said.

"The junior from GSA?!" Aggie gasped. "Amelia, way to go. You bagged yourself a baddie."

I hadn't actually met Markus Wayne yet, but Amelia stared off into the horizon so convincingly that I imagined she was daydreaming about him.

"Why did you think we would judge you?" I asked.

Amelia cleared her throat.

"Because he's. . . a furry," she said, almost whispering that last part.

We were all wearing headsets so the three of us could talk over the airplane noise.

"Oh honey, no. I'm not going to judge you for dating a furry. I'm just going to judge your date for being one," I said before Aggie raised an eyebrow at me.

Oh, right. I thought. *She'll drown me in the harbor if I give Amelia shit.*

But my bestie just snorted and laughed.

"Well, I think he's cute. And he's actually spent the last two years making his fursuit. I can appreciate a dedication to craft like that," Amelia said.

"What's his animal?" Aggie asked.

I scoffed.

"I think you mean 'fursona,' baby doll," I said.

The siren rolled her eyes and messed up my hair.

"It's a blue and green dog, actually," Amelia said. "But the way he listens to me go on and on about my hero's disappearance is sweet. And his parents are big-time trans rights supporters. One of them is a lawyer who helped a trans girl sue her school district here in Maine a few years ago over a bathroom case."

Aggie and I exchanged glances. That sounded pretty neat. Amelia hit the jackpot with her date which was all I wanted for her.

"What are you two doing for the afterparty?" Amelia suddenly asked, glancing over at us and taking the airplane down a couple hundred feet.

Aggie flashed me a wicked grin.

"I was going to give you a choice between swimming or coming back to my room and watching a terrible movie we could steal from my dad's DVD collection."

Raising an eyebrow, I asked, "Why would we purposefully choose a bad movie?"

My girlfriend leaned right up to my ear and said, "Well it's more fun to make out during a bad movie than a good movie. And who knows where the night would go after that?"

Heat rushed to my cheeks, and I swallowed nervously, picturing my girlfriend lying on the covers of her bed and inviting me to — nope! Not here. This is not the place for those kind of thoughts.

I shook my head to clear any less-than-chaste images from my mind.

"So what'll it be, Val? Swimming? Or a movie?"

Amelia stayed quiet while I tried not to sound too excited about watching a terrible movie with my girlfriend.

After that, our conversation turned toward the gowns we'd picked for the Snowflake Ball, and I lost myself in the normal queer life I'd dreamed of having for years. Ebeneazar had failed to rob me of my chosen future. I had two amazing moms at home waiting for me and a rather sweet demon who still owed me a favor. I wonder how he'd react to being called Uncle Arsyn.

Here we are again with another book finished and more queer characters in love. This story was quite a detour for me that all originated thanks to a few vampire novels I'd read this year (especially The Witch and The Vampire by Francesca Flores). Exit Eden's cover of "A Question of Time" also played a part in this story's creation.

You know how when you listen to music your brain will make scenes of a video to go along with the song? And most of the time it's anime. What, that's just me? Well, fuck. I'm a weirdo, I guess.

Anyway, I kept replaying the image of a cult trying to brainwash a girl and failing because she was just too stubborn. She'd eventually be rescued by a monster and go on to live a happy life.

If you've read my Raven Court Chronicles books, you know that benevolent monsters (like Varella) are a trope for me. When you're let down by enough regular humans in your life, you start to imagine superhuman beings that won't do the same thing. Yeah, welcome to my head. It's an entertaining party.

I love women, found family, and healing broken hearts. So, of course, this book will have plenty of those in it. And I hope you enjoy it all.

So weird to think Christmas is right around the corner. How many authors finish up vampire stories during the holiday season? Guess I should ask Sonia Hartl if I'm ever lucky enough to meet her one day.

In my last note, I told you that I was leaving my day job which was hurting my mental health. Well, I did that. And I'm happy to report I'm feeling much better now.

With this book finished, all that remains in 2023 is for me to celebrate Christmas with my darling wife and get ready for a little vacation. We'll be traveling up to Montreal to see a few friends and deliver late Christmas gifts. I'm excited because we're taking the train, and I love riding on trains. In fact, this will be my first international train trip! Woo!

It seems like the last time I wrote you readers an afterword I was also getting ready for a trip to see friends. Huh. Funny how that works.

Next on my writing agenda is to pivot back to the Raven Court Chronicles. Sometime in the next few days, I intend to start writing A Bargain for Wings. So get ready to say hello to your favorite werewolf and faerie queen once more, along with a couple of new faces.

As always, be sure to join my Discord if you want the latest updates on my writing. Who knows? Maybe the next Afterword I write will be me preparing for another trip. Ireland would be fun. (But you would all have to buy this book to make that trip happen).

In the meantime, eat more pizza. Build a snow-girl. Read by the fire with a cup of hot cocoa.

Later, bub.

• Autumn

ABOUT AUTUMN

Autumn Wolff is a woman of few simple interests. When she's not writing stories about girls kissing each other, Autumn is likely reading stories about girls kissing each other, playing Dungeons and Dragons, riding her bike, or watching a movie. She and her wife live near the ocean and consume more pizza than four turtles mutated by ooze. Autumn may not have the biggest living space, and it may never have enough bookshelves, but it's home.